Julep O'Toole

What I Really
Want to Do Is
Direct

Julep O'Toole

What I Really
Want to Do Is Direct

Trudi Trueit

DUTTON CHILDREN'S BOOKS

DUTTON CHILDREN'S BOOKS A division of Penguin Young Readers Group
Published by the Penguin Group • Penguin Group (USA) Inc., 375 Hudson Street,
New York, New York 10014, U.S.A. • Penguin Group (Canada), 90 Eglinton Avenue
East, Suite 700, Toronto, Ontario, Canada M4P 2Y3 (a division of Pearson Penguin
Canada Inc.) • Penguin Books Ltd, 80 Strand, London WC2R 0RL, England •
Penguin Ireland, 25 St Stephen's Green, Dublin 2, Ireland (a division of Penguin
Books Ltd) • Penguin Group (Australia), 250 Camberwell Road, Camberwell,
Victoria 3124, Australia (a division of Pearson Australia Group Pty Ltd) • Penguin
Books India Pvt Ltd, 11 Community Centre, Panchsheel Park, New Delhi - 110 017,
India • Penguin Group (NZ), Cnr Airborne and Rosedale Roads, Albany, Auckland 1310,
New Zealand (a division of Pearson New Zealand Ltd) • Penguin Books (South Africa)
(Pty) Ltd, 24 Sturdee Avenue, Rosebank, Johannesburg 2196, South Africa • Penguin
Books Ltd, Registered Offices: 80 Strand, London WC2R 0RL, England

For Debbie, my diamond

Contents

1 The Princess and the Pest

"Julep, dear, where is your heart?"

Julep glanced down at her black ballet-style shoes, each with a dainty baby-blue heart embroidered on the toe. "Huh?"

The stick figure of a drama teacher scurried toward the cafeteria stage. The heels of her mules went *smick-smack* against the checkerboard tiles. "Emotion, dear. I'm talking about emo-o-o-o-o-tion." When making a point, Mrs. Picklehaupt had a tendency to draw out the second syllable of important words. "Let's try it again. This time, Julep, don't merely read the lines; put some feeling into them. Think about what you're saying. Here is your handsome prince." She threw out a pale, bony arm and her peacock-print scarf slid off one shoulder. "You've waited all your life for him. Look at him. Smile at him. Ado-o-o-o-ore him."

Julep's amber eyes rolled skeptically to the right. Her Prince Charming, the one she'd waited for her entire life, was picking pieces of black licorice out of his teeth. And flicking them at her. Calvin also had a bag of licorice bits stuffed in the pocket of his jeans. Whenever the drama teacher wasn't watching, he'd launch a tiny square at her head. Julep didn't even want to think about how many black cubes were stuck in her kinky mass of reddish-brown hair.

Was Mrs. Picklehaupt completely out of her gourd? With his uneven buzz cut and a mouth dirtier than his ragged fingernails, Calvin Kapinski was nobody's true love. Least of all Julep O'Toole's. He existed only to make each day of her eleven years on Earth as miserable as possible. Calvin was getting so good at tormenting her Julep was pretty sure he was earning credit for it this semester.

"Yeah," said Calvin, waggling a black tongue at her. "Adore me."

"Eat fire ants."

"Now, is that any way to talk to your prince?" Calvin snapped his index finger against his thumb. Julep flinched as a fleck of licorice he'd plucked from between his front teeth landed on the sleeve of her mint-green dragonfly shirt.

"Jerk and a half," she growled, brushing away the goo. It left behind a black streak, which only grew larger when Julep tried to scrub it with a little saliva.

Biting back tears, Julep stared at the floor. She didn't want Calvin or any of the other kids waiting to audition to know how upset she was. She shouldn't even be here trying out for a part in *The Princess and the Pea*. It should never have happened. One minute you're getting a B-minus in second-period English and things are going pretty good. (Well, as good as they get for a middle child whose parents have been known to forget to pick her up from trumpet lessons.) Three quizzes, two essays, and an oral report later, you've dropped to a C-minus. You're so desperate to bring up your grade you'll do anything for extra credit, even agree to be in the school play. Painting scenery was one thing. Having to pretend to be in love with the most disgusting boy in the sixth grade, well . . .

. . . the C-minus was looking better all the time.

It occurred to Julep, as she stood beside a certain pest of a prince armed with edible ammunition, that this was probably how most students got involved in drama—by force. Nobody but an overachiever like Bernadette Reed could possibly consider acting fun. Julep squinted against the row of overhead lights, searching the Heatherwood Middle School cafeteria for any sign of her co-best friend. The honor-society officers meeting had ended ten minutes ago (Bernadette was vice president of the sixth-grade class). Where was she?

Her eyes slowly roving from left to right, Julep finally spotted Bernadette's waist-length mane of dark chocolate hair. Wearing a short jean skirt and a white cotton puckered-front blouse, her friend was sitting at the last table in the first row, though *sitting* was hardly the term for it. Bernadette was bouncing on the bench, tapping the heels of her sandals against the floor, and drumming her fingers on the table. That was the difference between them. Bernadette couldn't wait to get up here, while Julep couldn't wait to escape. Julep had always done her best to avoid things where you couldn't be certain of the outcome. Surprise endings were dangerous. They opened the door for you to humiliate yourself, or worse, be humiliated by someone else.

When their eyes met, Bernadette stopped moving long enough to give Julep a thumbs-up. "Good job," she mouthed, pushing her gold, rectangular, wire-frame glasses up higher on the bridge of her nose.

Julep answered with a feeble wave. Bernadette was sweet, but the pained expressions on the faces of everyone around her told the real story. Julep's acting deserved a big flush down one of the automatic toilets in the girls' bathroom.

Woooooosh!

Julep *was* trying to do what Mrs. Picklehaupt instructed. But she didn't get it. How was a person supposed to feel things they didn't actually feel, and say things they didn't actually think of? Acting was ridiculous. However, it *was* her only hope of raising her grade in Mr. Lee's English class. And so Julep stayed, doing her best to dodge the hail of black candy that flew her way.

Mrs. Picklehaupt paused to chat with eighth-grader Cherry Anne Oakes, the most famous actress in school. Last year, Cherry Anne had done a television commercial for bug spray. Only one role in *The Princess and the Pea* had already been cast. Cherry Anne was going to be the narrator. The news had come as a surprise. Everyone had assumed Cherry Anne would automatically be chosen for the princess, but a few days ago word had gotten out that Heatherwood's best actress had landed a good part in a *real* play at the Community Playhouse. Someone had overheard Cherry Anne tell Mrs. Picklehaupt that she still wanted to be in the school play, but would prefer a smaller, less demanding part. Translation: the juicy role of the princess was up for grabs. Julep could tell every girl in the cafeteria was drooling after it—every girl but her, of course.

4

Mrs. Picklehaupt was settling into her chair at the back of the cafeteria. She held up her clear, turquoise clipboard, a signal she was ready for Calvin and Julep to go again. Taking a shallow breath, Julep tried to calm her Jell-O knees. She wasn't good at public speaking, or public anything for that matter. Whenever she had to get up in front of people, Julep's hands began to sweat. Her fingertips went numb. Her eyes had trouble focusing. Her stomach would—

Oh, no! The corn chips she'd gulped down ten minutes ago were doing backflips in her digestive tract. Julep cleared her throat. Calvin let out a long, low burp. Julep took three small steps to the left. Calvin copied her, but took larger steps to close the distance between them.

"Zit Head," she muttered.

"Pooky bear." Calvin made smooching sounds.

Julep gagged, the taste of corn chips coming back to haunt her. She couldn't do this. She could NOT do this.

The sooner you say it, the sooner you can go home and take a boiling hot shower to wash off the Calvin germs.

She could do this.

Julep shielded herself with the script so she wouldn't have to look at *him*. "I know I'm sopping wet from the storm," she said, her voice quivering. "But you must believe me when I tell you that I am far more than I appear. Truly, I am a real . . . I am a real . . . whoa!"

The Princess and the Pea script had leaped from Julep's moist hands. She tried to get it back, but the pair of stapled pages had already caught the breeze from an open window. They fluttered just out of her reach. "One sec," Julep cried. "I'll . . . I'll get it, Mrs. Picklehaupt. Hold on . . ." She tripped across the stage, trying to tune out the snickers coming from the cafeteria. A few feet above Julep's head, her script was happily riding the mini–jet stream. It did several impressive loop-di-loops, giving Julep the chance to scamper across the stage to get ahead of it. Crouching, she waited until the script was directly above her. Then, at the precise moment it came down on the bottom half of a loop, she propelled herself skyward. Julep stretched out her arm, grunted, and grabbed . . . grabbed . . .

Air.

Julep landed on the outside edge of her leather ballet slipon, rolling her foot under her. Fire shot up the side of her ankle. She collapsed onto the wood floor. Nearing the red velvet curtain at the edge of the stage, the script was losing wind power. It did a slow downward spiral toward the floor. With a groan, Julep got up and limped forward. Gasping, she bent over and snatched up the script. She looked up, barely able to see through a thick cloud of reddish-brown bangs.

Calvin towered over her. "You were saying?"

"Truly I am a . . . a . . ." She tried to catch her breath. "I am a . . ."

"Klutz?" he finished.

The place erupted in laughter.

A rosy glow began to warm the eighty-seven freckles sprinkled over Julep's nose and cheeks. Her right temple began to itch, a sign of her growing anger. Pushing a clump of hair from her eyes, she scrambled to her feet.

"I'm a princess," she shouted, scratching her head. "A prin-CESS. Got it?" Her voice boomed out into the cafeteria. Julep balled up her fists. "And if you think I'm going to sleep on a bunch of old, crusty mattresses to prove it to a toad like you, forget it." She punched the air only a foot or so from Calvin's face. Calvin's gray coyote eyes doubled in size. His arms snapped up. And two licorice bits fell to the floor.

Fuming, Julep glared out at the audience. One drama teacher and thirty-one middle-school students were gaping at her. Millie Aldridge was madly scouring her script to find where *those* lines were written.

Loud enough for you, Mrs. Picklehaupt? Did it have enough feeling? Enough emo-o-o-otion? Enough HEART?

It took all of her effort not to say it out loud. Hands on her hips, Julep waited for the criticism that was sure to come. But Mrs. Picklehaupt didn't say a word. Instead, she tossed aside her clipboard and scurried from the auditorium as rapidly as her pointy mules would go.

"Mrs. P.?" called Cherry Anne, hurrying after her.

"I'm going to need a new partner," Calvin tossed into the crowd. Now recovered, he turned to sneer at Julep. "Mine's cracked."

That did it!

Julep threw her script at him. Racing down the front steps of the stage, she sped for the side door of the cafeteria. She felt everybody's eyes on her.

Keep it together. Hold on. You're almost there.

Soon, she would push her way to freedom and fresh air.

Soon, this whole nightmare would be over and she would never again have to do anything so unpredictable. Stupid extra-credit points.

Marching across the tile floor, her arms pumping for maximum speed, Julep realized there was a problem directly ahead of her—four of them actually. Danica Keyes, the most popular girl in the sixth grade, and her tagalong friends, Betsy Foster, Jillian Winters, and Kathleen O'Halleran, had circled their folding chairs in front of the side door. They were blocking her path. Their slouched postures indicated they had no plans to move. When Julep approached, Danica cupped her hands around her mouth. "Ladies and gentleman, Julep O'Toole: fairy-tale princess or professional wrestler? You decide." Her three friends cackled as if it were the most hilarious comment ever made.

Julep did not say a thing. Or make eye contact. However, she did pause long enough to bend forward over their camp and shake her terra-cotta head as hard as she could. A storm of black licorice rained down on the girls. They screamed. But they scattered. Julep kicked past a chair and slammed her body into the door handle. When, at last, she felt the late-afternoon sun on her face, Julep took her first normal breath in an hour. It felt wonderful to fill her lungs. And get the corn chips inside her to quit doing somersaults.

Unlocking her bicycle from the rack behind the gym, Julep felt her shoulders begin to relax. She had to admit the experience wasn't a complete fiasco. The look on Calvin's face after she'd gone bonkers on him was almost worth the humiliation. Almost. In truth, Julep hadn't meant to blow up like that. Her outburst had surprised even her. But Calvin had pushed her too far. He really ought to have known better. Never, never mess with a princess who's having a bad day. Julep hopped on her bike and coasted down the gravel path.

Huh.

Maybe there was something to this acting thing, after all.

2 Preteen Drama Queen

ow was your audition?"

"I survived," Julep said crisply, keeping her eyes on the page. She was lying on her stomach, her chin in her palms. Julep had propped up her library book between the back of her pillow and the white picket-fence headboard her dad had made for her tenth birthday.

Harmony's silver-blue eyes turned into slits. "What happened?"

"Scoot." Julep waved her sister away from the bed. "I have to finish *The Secret Garden* and write a book report tonight."

In theory, she would need to do exactly thirteen book reports, worth one hundred points each, if she hoped to bring her C-minus up to a B-minus in English. Even if she could somehow magically accomplish it, Mr. Lee wasn't likely to count *all* of them toward her grade. Otherwise, a person could simply skip doing their English homework for a whole year and turn in a gazillion book reports, instead. Hmm.

As usual, Harmony paid no attention to Julep's request. She was now stretched out beside her younger sister on the buttercup-yellow comforter. Beautiful, popular, and smart sisters, who were born three years ahead of you, rarely did anything you asked them to do. Yet they expected *you* to do everything they told you. It was, in Julep's view, S.N.F. (so not fair).

Harmony laid her sun-streaked head on the pillow, which made Julep's carefully balanced book topple to the floor. "Did you do everything I told you?" she asked.

See?

Julep collapsed face-first into her side of the pillow. "Yes," came her muffled reply.

"Did you stand up straight? Speak out? Not eat anything beforehand?"

"Yes, yes, and yes," lied Julep, a dozen acrobatic corn chips flipping through her brain.

"And you remembered to read your lines with feeling?"

If one more person said the word *feeling* to her, Julep was going to explode. *Ka-boom!* When the smoke cleared, all that would be left of her was one scorched mother-of-pearl bracelet watch and a smoldering pair of dalmation-print socks with pink faux-fur trim.

"Yeah," said Julep, recalling Calvin's stunned expression. "I said it with feeling all right." She didn't tell her sister *which* feeling.

"Then you're sure to get a main part."

"I don't want a main part. I'd rather be on the stage crew."

"The crew?" Harmony was aghast. "You're only saying that because you've never been up in front of a live audience."

Here it comes. Miss Fabulous is going to blab on and on and on about when she was in the sixth grade . . .

"When I was in the sixth grade . . ."

She was voted the best actress in her class.

"I was voted most likely to become a Hollywood star."

Why, she was cast over a bunch of older kids as the lead in Little Orphan Annie.

"Did you know I beat out three eighth graders to win the starring role in *Pollyanna?*"

Whatever. In conclusion, Harmony's touching performance earned her a standing ovation from the audience and two dozen red roses from the drama club.

"I got two standing ovations and a dozen yellow roses," said Harmony.

Close enough. And she lived happily ever after. The end. Please let it be the end.

"It was incredible," her sister said dreamily. "You don't forget something like that."

Not that you'd ever let me.

"Don't worry. Mrs. Picklehaupt will give you a decent part. After all, you are my sister. Besides, who is more dramatic than you? You're the queen."

"The princess, actually," Julep mumbled, closing her eyes.

Perhaps things weren't as fatal as she'd thought. Maybe Harmony was right. Julep did have a natural flair for creating drama wherever she went. And she had certainly given Mrs. Picklehaupt a riveting demonstration of her ability to tap into her emo-o-o-o-o-tions. Perhaps she had some acting talent, after all. And if you have talent, even a teaspoonful, you should not ignore it.

Without so much as a gurgle of fear in her stomach (or a single corn chip), Julep sees herself step onto the dimly lit Heatherwood cafeteria stage. A hush falls over the standing-room-only crowd. In ragged clothes and wet hair, Julep plays the lost princess who no one believes is royalty. Only after she is sensitive enough to feel the pea hidden beneath twenty mattresses and twenty feather beds is her prince (who, by the way, is NOT Calvin) convinced of her true identity. Julep's performance is tender, touching, and most of all, jam-packed with emo-o-o-o-o-tion. When the play ends, Julep gets not one, not two, but FIFTEEN standing ovations. Mrs. Picklehaupt smick-smacks across the stage in her mules to thrust four dozen yellow roses in her arms. "You have the most heart of any actress I've ever known, Julep," she gushes loudly enough for Harmony and their parents to hear. Julep is voted the best actress in the history of Heatherwood Middle School, the tristate area, and a good chunk of western Canada. The Snohomish News Journal prints a photo of her, along with a glowing review of the play, in its entertainment section. Steven Spielberg reads about her breathtaking performance and casts her in his next movie with Orlando Bloom. She wins an Oscar for the role. Julep gives a beautiful acceptance speech at the Academy Awards while, outside the theater, Calvin Kapinski is pelted with millions of black licorice bits by the entire North American branch of the Julep O'Toole fan club. It is perfect. Julep is perfect. Life is perfect . . .

Could it happen? Was there even a sliver of a chance that she might actually get a part in *The Princess and the Pea*? For the first time since her disastrous audition, Julep felt a microscopic speck of hope.

When Julep opened her eyes it was dark outside. Harmony was gone. There was a little wet spot on the pillow next to Julep's head. She had been drooling in her sleep. Yuck-o. Sitting up, Julep told herself she was being silly to think that she would ever get a part in the school play. She certainly wasn't the legendary Harmony O'Toole or the willowy goddess Cherry Anne Oakes. Even if, by some miracle, she *did* a get a part, her fear of public speaking was sure to doom her. She'd never be able to stand up in front of hundreds of people and say her lines without:

A. Throwing Up

B. Hyperventilating

C. Fainting

D. Any combination of the above. If Julep was smart, she'd stick to stage crew, do the minimum work required to earn her extra credit, and scram the moment Mr. Lee entered her B-minus into the computer. Nothing bad would happen if she stuck to safe stuff like xeroxing scripts and building sets. Of course, nothing good was bound to happen either. But Julep tried not to think about that.

6:20 P.M.   Mood: Bummed

Dear Amelia:

I am mega-sorry. It's been nineteen days since I wrote in you! I promise never to stay away so long again. M.C.H. (see decoder page in my <u>locked</u> music box).

I auditioned for the school play today. I made the drama teacher sick (Cherry Anne heard Mrs. Picklehaupt throwing up in the staff bathroom). However, I did get even with Danica and her popular crowd. Did I mention it's cloudy today with a 100 percent chance of licorice rain? I.L.H.

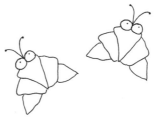

I have to go! Mom is barking at me to practice my trumpet (woof, woof). I can play low C, D, E, and sometimes F and G (though it makes me dizzy).

My mother is making artichoke pastry puffs for dinner. Artichokes have the perfect name 'cause they make me choke! Time to put P.N.T. into action. It never fails!

   C.Y.L.,

   Julep Antoinette O'Toole

Julep's Decoder Page
IS THIS <u>YOUR</u> JOURNAL?   I THINK NOT!!

M.C.H.: Middle Child's Honor

I.L.H.:   Insert Laugh Here!

P.N.T.: Plan Number Three:

Step One: Wear lemon–lime striped cardigan with big side pockets to dinner.

Step Two: Slip Mom's cooking off my plate and into pockets.

Step Three: After dinner, run down to the pond behind our house.

Step Four: Hurl food into pond where it can never harm anyone.

C.Y.L.: Check You Later

3   The More Girl

What do you think?"

Repelled, yet slightly fascinated, Julep leaned across the table to examine the contents of the freezer bag. Inside the plastic, dozens of lumpy squares, bent triangles, thin disks, and other various shapes bobbed in a polluted pea-green sea. There was only one logical conclusion. "Science project?"

"Snack." A grin spread across Trig Maxwell's face. "It's my new concoction. You throw in some jalapeño chips, sliced pepperoni, marshmallows, dried apples and raisins, and a carton of guacamole dip. Then you shake it up and ta-da." He opened the seal, dipped his hand into the light green ooze, and pulled out what had once been a normal white marshmallow. Now, marinated in lukewarm guacamole muck, it looked like an alien parasite—an alien parasite with a gloppy slice of pepperoni attached to its head. Yuck-o. Trig popped it into his mouth. "Supreme," he said, licking his thumb. He thrust the bag at her. "Want some?"

"No! I . . . uh, I brought lunch, thanks," she said politely, hoping he hadn't seen the giant tremor that had just zapped her from head to toe.

Julep dumped the contents of her paper bag onto the table: an avocado, lettuce, and tomato sandwich, a bag of carrot chips, and an orange. Not too heinous considering her mom, a vegetarian, sometimes gave her odd stuff like fried tofu squares or wild-mushroom-and-bean-curd wraps. Julep, who was not a vegetarian, didn't like weird food. Trig, by contrast, could eat anything. And did. What never failed to astonish Julep was the many ways he could mix and match food you wouldn't dare combine to make things, well, only he would dare consume. Once, he devised a peanut-butter-and-marmalade pizza, which wouldn't have been so bad but for the Cocoa Krispies sprinkled on top. Ew. Then there were the raw-cookie-dough bars frosted with ranch salad dressing and sunflower seeds. Double ew. Julep's personal favorite, and the ultimate in ew-ness, was the picnic shake. It involved stuffing a cooked hot dog, bun, and the condiments of your choice (mustard, ketchup, pickles, etc.) in a blender and thrashing it on high speed. In under a minute, perfectly good food was transformed into a chunky, puke-brown sludge that nobody but Trig would dream of eating. Okay, Julep's seven-year-old brother, Cooper, had tried it, too. But given that Cooper considered dryer lint an appetizer, that wasn't saying much.

Julep had started to peel her orange when she heard her name echo through the cafeteria. Bernadette was flying through the room, her long mocha hair and lilac sweater-coat flying out behind her. She dodged right, then left, to avoid kids in her way. "It's up," she shouted when she reached the head of their row. "Julep, it's up!" At that, everybody near them turned to look, including the Head Goose and her goslings (Trig's nickname for the ultrapopular Danica Keyes and her friends). Once

Danica, Betsy, Jill, and Kathleen saw that it was a mere mortal, they quickly went back to their salads, along with a heated debate over whether chain belts were a fashion "do" or "don't." Not that Julep had been eavesdropping.

Panting, Bernadette pulled up next to Trig. "Are you guys . . . huh . . . done?"

Julep pointed to the clock to remind her that just eight minutes of first lunch had passed.

Bernadette flopped down beside Trig. "Hurry, will you? *It's* up."

"What's up?" Trig crunched into a folded jalapeño chip dripping in guacamole.

"The list for—" Bernadette sniffed the air. Her wrinkled nose led her straight to Trig's freezer bag.

He offered it to her. Recoiling, Bernadette held her nose shut with two fingers.

Trig tossed his mop of overgrown, salsa-red hair. "No guts, huh? Or maybe you're jealous of my cooking?"

"Uh-huh," she said in a nasal voice. "I'm real jealous of your green globules of goop."

Trig stroked his chin. "Hey, I like that. Mind if I use it?"

"It's all yours. Just keep that gunk a mile away from me."

"Trig's Globules of Goop," he said thoughtfully. "This could be the recipe I enter in the Young Chefs of America contest."

"I hate to remind you," said Bernadette, reluctantly releasing her nose, "but your bizarre-o concoctions have lost in the first round every year since third grade. Give it up, Maxwell. Nobody wants to eat salami ice cream or deep-fried oatmeal or any other stinky thing you invent."

"How would you know? Lots of people like my original recipes."

Rummaging through her backpack, Bernadette brought out her lunch. "You mean, like the judges who quit last year after you fed them tuna-fish lollipops?"

"Suckers. And they did not quit."

"Did so."

"Did not."

"Tell him, Julep."

"Tell *her,* Julep."

"They didn't quit." Julep said from behind a neat pile of orange rinds. "They got sick, remember?"

"Oh, yeah," her friends said in unison.

"I almost made the finals with that one," Trig said wistfully. "If only my tuna hadn't dropped to room temperature."

There was a moment of silence for Trig's spoiled fish on a stick. It was broken by the sound of Bernadette popping the top off her minican of Pringles. Julep pried apart her orange only to get squirted in the eye with a shot of juice. "Ahh!" she yelped, blinking rapidly.

"Heads up," said Trig, his voice edged with fear.

Julep was busy rubbing away the stinging citrus liquid. "Huh?"

"Monster alert," cried Bernadette.

"Where?" squealed Julep, a finger still in her eye. Nobody was answering! *"Where?"*

"Your row, Julep. Watch your back."

If only she could!

Mrs. Flaskin, the lunch monitor, or Lunch Monster, as she

was known throughout Heatherwood, was notorious for snatching food from innocent students. Weighing well over three hundred pounds, Mrs. Flaskin wore calico-print sack dresses, thick mud-brown support hose, and black orthopedic shoes. She rarely spoke. She never smiled. The Lunch Monster tottered up and down the aisles during each lunch period. Her good eyeball (the other was glass, or so the rumor went) panned from side to side, ferreting out any unprotected food. Cupcakes, corn dogs, cookies, even rice cakes—nothing was safe from her bulbous purple hands. For a hefty woman, she had incredible reflexes. Mrs. Flaskin could pluck a pudding cup off your tray faster than you could cry "tapioca!"

Today, the Lunch Monster was wearing a sapphire-blue dress covered in tiny yellow buttercups. Julep, who was quite skilled at guessing games, figured there had to be at least forty thousand flowers on that dress. In the fourth grade, she'd won an enormous jar of colored jelly beans on Valentine's Day for estimating how many beans were inside it (without going over). Julep had guessed 1,999. There were 2,140 (for the date February 14, of course). Everyone else in her class had guessed in the hundreds, but Julep knew it wasn't that low. There was a trick to it. She'd learned a long time ago that such games were optical illusions. There was always far more in the jar than you expected. Whatever your mind told you was inside, double it. Julep calculated there were 42,675 buttercups on that dress (without going over).

The moment Bernadette sounded the alarm, the three of them rushed to eat, cover, and/or hide their lunches. Julep threw her orange halves, chips, and sandwich into her sack.

Bernadette slid her Pringles can into her lap. Trig started shoveling Green Globules of Goop into his mouth at Mach speed. Her heart pounding and her eye watering, Julep hunkered down. Soon, thick, raspy breathing told her the Lunch Monster was directly behind her.

Julep knew from the terrified look on Trig's face that the Lunch Monster's evil eye had locked onto his latest concoction. Trig's mouth was so full, he was helpless to defend himself. All he could do was shake his head and say, "Nah-wah-thuth."

Frozen to her bench, Julep felt a dark shadow loom over her. She caught a strong whiff of onion rings. A mammoth buttercup-dotted blue curtain descended next to her. Out of the corner of her eye, Julep saw a ripple of blubber. This couldn't be happening. The Lunch Monster was going to swipe Trig's Green Globules of Goop! Watching the tsunami of arm fat roll from side to side, and the swollen fingers deftly move toward their prey, Julep knew she needed to do something. And fast. But what? What could one eighty-pound girl possibly do to beat the enormous fire-breathing food-sucking Lunch Monster?

"Wait!" Julep threw out an arm, knocking the Lunch Monster's hand away seconds before it would have closed around Trig's bag. Julep beat back the folds of fabric suffocating her and staggered to her feet. Julep stared up into the volcanic eyes of the Lunch Monster—not an easy task since one of those eyes had wandered away to check out the ice-cream stand. "You don't want that," hollered Julep.

"No?" An evil growl came from the depths of the buttercups. "Why not?"

That's when Julep hit her with the most powerful weapon she had. "Because it's sugar-free."

The Lunch Monster shuddered, and 42,675 cute yellow flowers waved at Julep. Running her pudgy fingers through her short crop, the Monster glowered at Trig. He had turned to stone. The mammoth arm pulled away. The Monster retreated. The last thing they heard was the annoying squeak of two orthopedic shoes. Slightly woozy, Julep sank into her seat. Nobody said a word until the Lunch Monster was two full rows away.

"Close call," whispered Bernadette.

"Uh-huh," said Trig, his eyes bulging.

Bernadette gave Julep an admiring smile. "I can't believe you did that."

Julep couldn't believe it either.

"I heard she eats anything," said Bernadette. "Even dog biscuits."

"She probably gets them from Calvin," said Julep.

The girls snickered.

Trig said, "Uh-huh."

"I heard she never smiles because she has no teeth," said Julep.

"That would explain her thing for pudding cups." Bernadette poured the last broken bits of Pringles into her hand. "So can we go now?"

"Where?"

"The drama room, of course. Mrs. Picklehaupt posted the cast and crew list for the play."

"It's up? Why didn't you tell me?"

Bernadette let out a shriek, nearly choking on her chips.

"Ohhhhh," Julep said, finally catching on. "Let's go. I'll eat on the way." She stood up. "Trig, are you coming?"

"Uh-huh," he said, but didn't move.

Bernadette waved a hand in front of his face. "I think he's in shock."

"That or the Green Globules of Goop aren't sitting well."

"Trig?" Bernadette said his name as if speaking to a toddler. "We're going to the drama room. We'll be back in five, okay?"

"Uh-huh."

Outside Mrs. Picklehaupt's room, Bernadette and Julep had to wait behind a bunch of seventh-grade boys, who were taking forever to check the postings. The drama teacher had tacked two pink pages onto the bulletin board in the hallway. Julep could see that one piece of paper read CAST and the other said CREW, but that was about all she could see. Seventh-grade guys sure had big heads. At last, the students ambled away and Bernadette slipped in to stand as close to the bulletin board as she could without touching it. She began scanning the CAST page.

Julep looked, too, though she did not get face-to-cork with the board. Nor did she whimper, "Oh, please, oh, please, oh, please . . ." the way her co-best friend was doing.

It was better to remain calm, even a bit disinterested, in situations like this. No sense letting everyone witness your disappointment when you didn't get a part. Besides, all Julep needed to do was make it onto the stage crew and she was home free—English-wise, anyway.

Stage crew. Stage crew. Stage crew.

Stage crew. Stage crew. Stage crew.

Julep kept repeating the phrase in her head until she was saying it faster and faster and faster in sync with her quickening heartbeat.

"Eeeeek!" Suddenly Bernadette's arms were around her. "I'm the queen, the prince's mother. She has lots of lines, you know." She pulled back, her brown eyes wide. "I got a big part on my very first try. Isn't that something?"

"It's great," Julep said, but her voice fell to the floor with a lifeless *splat*. It wasn't that Julep wasn't thrilled for her co-best friend. She was. Sort of. It was only that Bernadette Reed never failed at anything. Never! Between the two of them, Bernadette was more brilliant, more athletic, more creative, more musical, more outgoing—the girl was more of everything. And when you aren't much of anything, hanging around someone who *is* plenty of something can sure wear you down. Julep wished that for once she could be the More Girl. Just once.

"Let's check for you." Bernadette began running her finger down the page.

But Julep had already found her name. It was on the bottom of the list marked CREW. She was dead last again. She forced a smile, forced herself to say enthusiastically, "Here I am. I'm on the crew. All right!"

Bernadette dropped her hand. "Oh," she said. Failing was bad enough, but being on the receiving end of Bernadette's pity, yet again, would be a thousand times worse. So Julep pretended not to notice her friend's sympathetic face. She also pretended she hadn't seen Calvin's name on the CAST list.

Okay, he was Villager Number Five, but still, it was a part. How degrading. Licorice Boy had beat her out.

"It's going to be great." Julep swallowed past the jawbreaker-size lump in her throat. "I can't wait to start. Really," she insisted when Bernadette's right eyebrow inched upward. "It'll be a blastoid to build sets and paint scenery. It's really, *really* what I wanted."

Wasn't it?

As they stood there, Betsy Foster, a.k.a. Gosling Number One, came out of the girls' bathroom. Beyond the swinging door, Julep heard a toilet flush.

Woooooosh!

And just like that a dream was gone.

7:39 P.M.   Mood: Blah

Dear Amelia:

I made drama club. I'm on the S.C., which is ~~probably~~ definitely a good thing. No gymnastic corn chips for me!

My sister is more steamed than Mom's spinach. She says even a small part would have been better than S.C. She says I am shaming the family name. I say S.M.S.F., Harmony!!

Dad hugged me and said he was proud of me for getting involved at school. I didn't tell him I would never have done it if I hadn't desperately needed the E.C. points. It would only hurt us both. Did I tell you? Danica Keyes gets to be the princess. People with: 1) great hair, 2) designer clothes, and 3) ZERO freckles get everything they want. Not that I care.

C.Y.L,

Julep

P.S. I think S.C. is going to be fun, don't you? It's going to be the best best <u>BEST</u> thing ever!

Julep's Decoder Page

IF YOU'RE READING THIS YOU'RE IN <u>BIG</u> TROUBLE

S.C.:	Stage Crew
S.M.S.F.:	Smell My Stinky Feet
E.C.:	Extra Credit (duh)

THAT MEANS YOU, COOPER MAYNARD O'TOOLE!

4 The Spy in Stall Six

That's supposed to be an enchanted tree? Looks more like a lopsided tornado to me."

Julep, sitting cross-legged on the floor near the back wall of the stage, crushed a brown square of tissue paper in her fist. "Scram, Bath Scum."

Amazingly, the most obnoxious boy in the sixth grade did not insult her back, although before slithering away, he did pump his hand under his armpit to make a series of screeching noises. More amazingly, Julep didn't mind. At this point, any distraction from her monotonous work, even an arm-farting Calvin, was welcome.

For over an hour, Julep had been bent over a papier-mâché tree trunk balling up sheets of brown and gold tissue paper and gluing them on. Scrunch a piece of paper, dab it with the glue-soaked paintbrush, and stick it onto the wire frame covered with hardened newspaper. Over and over again she did it—scrunch, glue, stick.

Scrunch. Glue. Stick.

It was brutal. Julep's neck felt tighter than the twisty trunk.

Her foot was asleep. And the last two fingers on her left hand were now stuck together. How had *that* happened?

Stage crew was the WORST thing ever. For a whole week, the group had been slaving over papier-mâché trees and plants for the outside of the castle. The stage crew was made up mostly of sixth graders: Julep, Eddie Levitt (Calvin's best friend), Millie Aldridge, Robbie Cornfeld, and Kathleen O'Halleran. Gosling Number Three was less than delighted to learn she would not be quacking lines onstage with her three friends. Oh, and Trig, too. Like Julep, he had come up short a few E.C. points in English. Unlike Julep, Trig had managed to avoid auditioning with Mrs. Picklehaupt. Julep hadn't bothered to ask how he'd done it. When it came to teachers, Trig had special powers of persuasion. With his soft Kentucky drawl, which grew thicker the more trouble he was in, he could charm his way out of anything—detention when he didn't have a hall pass, P.E. class when he didn't care to square-dance, and a test when he didn't want to study. The Teacher Charmer was currently lounging at an end table in the cafeteria. He was napping on the bench while Millie finished his papier-mâché rosebush. Typical.

Attaching clump number 1,981 (or was it 1,891?) of tissue to her mutant tree/tornado, Julep kept one eye on the front of the stage. Mrs. Picklehaupt was taking the actors through the scene where the princess arrives at the castle. Goslings Betsy Foster and Jillian Winters were huddled together near the wings waiting to answer the knock at the castle door. They played the queen's maids. Julep didn't understand that bit of casting. She had seen their auditions. Three words. Hid. E. Ous. You couldn't even hear Jillian when she spoke. Betsy sounded like a hostage reading her kidnapper's demands. Still, the two sixth graders had gotten decent parts in the play. It was so S.N.F. Julep wanted to skywrite it in red, white, and blue smoke above the city.

Scrunch. Glue. Stick.

Julep's head snapped up. Something had happened. Everyone onstage, including Bernadette, was now laughing. Danica had covered her face with her script. She must have flubbed a line. Ethan Thornquist, who was playing the role of the prince, put a hand on Danica's shoulder. He was semicute, meaning if Julep were interested in boys, which she wasn't, and if she had to pick a boyfriend, which she had no intention of doing, then Ethan might be a good choice. He was a math genius, too. The semicute, smart seventh grader said something and everybody, including Bernadette, laughed harder.

Scrunch. Glue. STICK.

The actors started reading again and got through most of the scene before Mrs. Picklehaupt stopped them with a flash of her turquoise fiberglass clipboard. "Did everyone catch that? Did everyone see how Bernadette paused there, and let her line flow? Don't rush your words, people. Relax, and let them come to you as naturally as if your brain were formulating them for the very first time. Exce-e-e-e-ellent work, Bernadette."

Scrunch. GLUE. STICK.

The actors picked up from where they had left off. It wasn't long before they came to *the* line, also known as Julep's line of destruction, or, simply, the L.O.D. "I know I'm sopping wet from the storm." Danica tugged on a long lock of satiny black hair, lingering on the delicate corkscrew curl at the end. "But you must believe me when I tell you that I am more than I appear. Truly," she cried, her voice breaking with despair, "I am a real princess."

Danica's performance was filled with emo-o-o-o-o-tion. It was tender and touching. Why, it was absolutely—

"Delightful," gushed Mrs. Picklehaupt. "Utterly deli-i-i-ightful, my dear."

SCRUNCH. GLUE. STICK!

"Julep?"

"What?"

"How's it going?" Tessa Garroway, the eighth grader in charge of set design, hovered over her.

"Fine," she murmured.

Tessa ran a hand through her short blond bangs. "Do you want to do something different?"

Julep flung her papier-mâché tree aside. "You bet."

Tessa grinned, revealing a set of pink braces. "You can help Kathleen sew slipcovers for the big foam-rubber pieces that we'll be using for the prop mattresses and feather beds. She's in the home-ec room." As Julep sprang to her feet, Tessa added, "When you've finished your tree, of course."

Julep crumbled.

"Funky fashion statement," Tessa said before strolling away.

Huh? Julep eyes traveled down the front of her burgundy lace tee and favorite pair of faded jeans. She had worn this outfit dozens of times and there wasn't anything remotely funky—

Then she saw it. The white cat on the ankle of her sock was sporting a brown-and-gold tissue-paper beard.

Good work, Julep. You just papier-mâchéd yourself.

After ten minutes of scrubbing her sock in the girls' bathroom, all Julep had to show for it were several shredded paper towels, an empty soap dispenser, and a sore elbow from where she'd fallen against the sink. Maybe she ought to have taken off the sock before trying to clean it. Her foot was sopping wet. The soapy paper towels she'd used had dissolved the tissue paper on contact, turning her beautiful white Persian into a dirty brown alley cat.

"Water-soluble glue, my foot," she muttered, then snorted at her own joke.

Julep shoved her palm against the silver button on the hand dryer. Clutching the sink for support, she stood on one leg and held her foot under the stream of lukewarm air. A minute later, when the dryer shut off, Julep still had a pretty soggy sock. She also had a bladder begging to be emptied.

Julep hobbled down the row of stalls, trying to keep her damp foot off the floor. She made a left turn at the second stall and headed down the row. The sixth and last stall was her favorite. It had the most privacy. The downside was it had a broken latch. You had to push the door with all your might to shut or, more accurately, wedge it into place. She also didn't like the so-called smart toilets they had in middle school, which were supposed to automatically flush when you were done, but tended to flush too early or too late or not at all. The red light above the toilet bothered her. It was like an eyeball, always watching you. When you were done, the eye began to blink to let you know the flush was coming. It kept on blinking until the flush cycle was over. Keeping to her motto, pee and pee quickly, Julep began unzipping her jeans. The *eee-yoh* squeak of the main door warned her that somebody was entering the girls' bathroom.

Rats!

Whizzing was one of those things a person should do alone whenever possible. Julep stood completely still, waiting until she could pee in peace.

". . . thought we agreed I was going to say the line."

"I didn't agree to anything."

"But you have four more lines that I do."

"What nimrod counts lines anyway?" Then a cackle. "I guess you do."

Double rats! It was Betsy and Jillian.

"Why don't you guys split it?"

And Kathleen. She was—how did Trig put it?—not the sharpest crayon in the box.

The goslings hadn't earned their nickname for nothing. They were quite the quackers. This could take a while. Relaxing, Julep leaned against the wall. It let out a groan. She froze.

"What was that?" asked Kathleen. "Did you guys hear that?"

"Is anybody in here?" called Jillian.

"Hell-o-o-o-o!"

Julep should have answered. It would have been so easy to cry out, "It's me, Julep." But she didn't. A moment later, the girls resumed their conversation.

"Since Mrs. Picklehaupt said we could choose who says the line, why don't we have Kathleen decide?" offered Betsy. "We'll each say it and Kathleen will pick a winner, okay?"

Jillian reluctantly agreed.

Betsy cleared her throat. "Follow me, please."

"Okay," replied Kathleen, "but weren't you going to do the line first?"

"That *is* the line, you dingleberry."

Julep let out a chortle, and had to clamp a hand over her mouth. She dropped her head, too, in case any sound squeezed through her fingers. A dirty brown cat winked at her. Oh, no! Her shoe! She had left it out there in plain sight. If the goslings saw the black leather slip-on with the little baby-blue heart on the toe, they would know it was hers. And they would know she was here. What if they flung open the door (though it would take all of them to do it) and accused her of spying? What then? Why hadn't Julep admitted she was in the bathroom when she'd had the chance? She *really* had to whiz now. She crossed one leg over the other and lightly bounced.

"My turn," announced Jillian, before saying, so softly Julep could barely hear, "Follow me, please."

"So who wins? Jillian or *me*?" Betsy's tone made it sound like more of a threat and less of a question.

"Uh . . . well, you were both good."

"But who was the *best*?"

"I'm not sure."

"Come on, Kathleen," sniped Betsy, "it's not like I was as awful as Bernadette."

Julep stiffened.

"Did you guys see the way Bernadette spits when she talks?"

"Did I?" Jillian squealed. "She nailed me twice. Once on the neck and once right on the side of my nose!"

The goslings' response hit Julep's ears in stereo. "Ewwww."

"I'm telling you right now, stand back if you have any lines with the Spit Chick," Betsy advised.

"Speaking of saliva," said Jillian. "Isn't it pathetic the way Danica drools all over Ethan?"

"I'm a princess, I'm a princess, oh, please, please believe me, my prince," mimicked Betsy. "I almost hurled my Ho Hos."

Jillian said that she, too, was one gag away from barfing baked goods.

"She so overacts," snapped Betsy. "The only reason she got the part was because of her long hair."

"I know. What an injustice."

"If my hair were past my shoulders, then that part would have been mine—"

Eee-yoh.

Somebody else was coming into the bathroom. Julep took bigger hops.

"Hey, Danica," cooed Jillian and Betsy.

"My lips are so dry," said Danica. "Does anyone have any lip balm?"

"I do," Betsy rushed to say.

"Me, too," echoed Jillian.

"Take mine," said Kathleen. "It's pineapple coconut."

"Mine's apple pie à la mode," shot Betsy.

Jillian piped up with, "I've got frosted cinnamon roll."

Julep's jaw dropped. Unbelievable! Seconds ago they were ripping their leader to bits. Now they were falling over one another to rescue her chapped lips.

"My hands are frozen," Danica said. "I'm so nervous about the play."

"You shouldn't be worried," said Betsy sweetly. "You're doing a great job."

"We were all saying how much we think so," added Jillian.

Liars! Big fat gosling liars! It was all Julep could do not to bust out of the stall and reveal the truth.

Danica sighed. "It's hard to remember everything Mrs. Picklehaupt tells you to do. You know, smile when you say this, walk over there when you say that, don't turn your back to the audience—it never ends. And we go off-script in another week."

"Where's off-script?"

"Not where. What." Danica explained to Kathleen it meant the actors could no longer use their scripts during rehearsals. "Everything has to be memorized."

"We'll help you learn your lines," said Jillian.

Betsy giggled. "Sure, we'd love to."

Julep stuck her tongue out at the wall closest to the girls. What phonies!

"Look at that," said Jillian. "Somebody left a crusty black shoe in here."

Julep sucked in a breath.

Leave it alone. And they are not *crusty. At least, not that particular pair.*

"It's wet, too. Yuck."

Go away. Drop my shoe and get out of here!

"I used to have a pair like these," said Kathleen. "Mine had shamrocks on the toes. And they had laces instead of a strap. And mine were suede instead of leather. And they were brown not black—"

"Goody for you," Betsy cut in. "Danica, are those new jeans?"

"Yeah. You like?"

"I love."

Thank you, Betsy, for changing the subject!

Jillian followed up with her usual, "Me, too."

"The tattooed vine down the leg is cute," said Kathleen. "Did you do it?"

"Uh, no, they come that way, Kathleen."

"They must have been expensive."

"Only two hundred."

Dollars? Was she serious? Julep pictured the rigid stare she'd get from her mother if she even joked about buying a pair of two-hundred-dollar jeans.

Eee-yoh.

"Danica, you want to come over to my house?" Betsy was asking. "I got a new line to say today and I could use some acting tips—?"

The door swung shut.

Julep counted to twenty before reaching for the door handle. Grabbing it with both hands, she yanked as hard as she could. The door popped open, smacking her in the chin. Julep poked her head out of the stall. She peered left. Then right.

All clear.

Julep hobbled to the sink, located her shoe, and stuffed her foot into it. She didn't bother fastening the strap. Not until she was limping across the cafeteria toward Bernadette, her damp foot squeaking with each step, did it occur to her that someone had put liquid soap in her shoe. Pink gel was oozing out around the strap.

Cute, goslings. Real cute.

Julep also realized that she had forgotten to pee. Oh, well. Some things were more important than a soapy foot. More important, even, than whizzing. This was definitely one of those things.

5   A Charmed Life

I'm quitting the play," Julep told Trig as they walked to school.

"Okay."

Julep counted off seventeen steps before she couldn't stand it any longer. "Don't you want to know why?"

"Nope." Trig, who was a head taller than she, didn't glance down. He was wearing his favorite Seattle Mariners baseball cap—backward, as usual, with a tuft of hair sticking out the hole in front.

"Oh. Well. Good." Julep shoved her hands into the pockets of her navy fleece vest with three monarch butterflies flitting across the right lapel. "Don't try to talk me out of it."

"Wouldn't dream of it."

No, of course he wouldn't. Trig not only understood quitting, he excelled at it.

"Cooper!" Julep shouted. "Wait for us at the corner."

From a half block ahead, her seven-year-old brother's creamy-blond head didn't swing around. Cooper kept kicking pebbles off the sidewalk, acting as if he hadn't heard her directions. But he did slow down, which meant he *had* heard.

"What are you going to say to Mrs. Picklehaupt?"

"How about, 'Mrs. Picklehaupt, I quit'?"

Trig let out a low whistle.

"What?"

"If you don't have a surefire excuse, she'll talk you out of it."

"She will not."

"Will so."

"Pretend I'm her. Go ahead." He motioned toward himself. "Prove me wrong."

Julep grinned. "Okay." This was going to be fun.

"Mrs. Picklehaupt," she said, lifting her chin. "I've decided to quit the play."

"But, Julep, my dear, we're all counting on you," he said, copying their drama teacher's melodic voice. Julep laughed. Trig, however, didn't crack up a bit. "We're depending on you for set design and to help during the play. You're part of a valu-u-u-u-able team."

"Yes, but—"

"I know you're disappointed about not being selected as an actor—"

"I am not." Her smile vanished. This wasn't the way it was supposed to go. And how did Trig know she had been upset about not getting a part anyway? Julep hadn't told anybody but her journal about that. "I am not," she said again, softer.

"Then what"—Trig paused to peer over an invisible clipboard—"is the matter?"

"See, I joined drama club for extra credit. I didn't realize how hard it would—"

"Are you saying the play isn't worth a bit of hard work?"

"What I meant was—"

"Are you saying you are in the habit of quitting when things get rough?"

"No, I—"

"Are you saying your promises don't mean anything?"

"I never—"

"Are you going to simply give up and let everyone down? Is that what you're trying to tell me, Julep O'Toole?" A pair of mossy-green eyes probed hers without so much as a single blink. They stared at each other for nearly half a minute, the tension-filled silence expanding with each passing second.

Julep was the first to snap their connection. "All right," she said, in surrender. "What do I say?"

While Trig mulled over his vast list of possible excuses, they continued up Bayview Avenue. "Let's see. An illness might work. How about an allergy? You could be allergic to—"

"Glue!" Julep jumped in. "We use tons of glue on the sets."

"No. A reason like that would only get you moved to something else, like painting or sewing. It has to be something where the only solution is for you to drop out of the play entirely."

"Okay, so what should I say?"

"I don't know."

"What do you mean you don't know?" Julep was starting to get panicky.

"I need to think about it."

"Don't take too long." Julep was not about to endure another afternoon tangling with the papier-mâché jungle. He promised he would get back to her by the end of second period. Breaking the news to Trig about her plans to bail on the play had gone reasonably well. But Julep had one more person to inform, and this one was not likely to go as smoothly.

"What do you mean you're quitting?" Bernadette flung her green English notebook on her desk. "You can't quit. We were going to do the play together, remember?"

Julep pressed her hands downward, signaling for her friend to reduce the volume a few decibels. She didn't want the students coming into Mr. Lee's classroom, especially the Head Goose and two of three goslings, to hear.

"You're doing fine without me," Julep rasped. "Besides, we hardly see each other. You're up onstage and I'm . . . well, not. You won't even know I'm gone."

Bernadette stuck out her lower lip.

"I'll miss you, too," said Julep.

"But you said you wanted to be on the stage crew. You said it was going to be great and that you couldn't wait to get started. You said it was going to be a blastoid to build sets and paint scenery. You said it was what you really *really*—"

"I know, I know."

Never become friends with someone who has a photographic memory and can regurgitate every single thing you've ever said with perfect recollection. It will haunt you forever.

Julep took her seat, which was in front of Bernadette's. Her co-best friend sat down, too. "Look," said Julep, spinning in her chair. "I glued my fingers together." She held up the fourth and fifth fingers of her left hand to prove that even now, two days after the fact, whenever they touched they *still* clung to each other. "That's not the worst of it. I had to work with Kathleen. You try sewing mattress covers with Gosling Number Three. I did four whole covers until I realized they were all too small."

Bernadette let out a tiny gasp.

"Kathleen said nobody told her we needed to measure the foam pieces *before* we cut the fabric." Julep crossed her eyes. "Bernadette, if I have to go through this for even one more day, I will turn into a cashew nut. I swear I will."

"I had no idea."

"Now you do."

"But if you quit, what will you do about—"

The tardy bell rang.

"—your extra credit?" she finished without missing a beat.

Julep glanced over her shoulder at Mr. Lee, who was at the head of their row taking roll. "I guess I'll get a C-minus."

It would be Julep's first C in middle school. Her parents weren't going to like it one bit. But maybe that was the way it was supposed to be. Maybe it was her destiny to be a C. Not extraordinary. Not hideous. Not memorable. Simply, average.

"This calls for some serious cheering up," whispered Bernadette. "You want to come over tonight and karaoke? You can be Kelly Clarkson on 'Behind These Hazel Eyes.'"

Julep gave her a grateful nod. Her friend always knew just what to say and just when to say it. Bernadette was her diamond. Rare and brilliant and constant.

Behind her, Bernadette was humming "Behind These Hazel

Eyes." Julep joined in. The girls kept humming, though very, very quietly, long after Mr. Lee started the lesson. With Kelly Clarkson still in her head a half hour later, Julep finished her grammar worksheet. Stretching her arms upward, she saw Betsy lean across the aisle to hand Danica a rope of red licorice. Taking it, Danica absently gazed back. Her sea-green eyes met Julep's amber ones. The little dimple in Danica's chin disappeared. She abruptly looked away.

Julep wasn't surprised. Her secret friendship—if you could call it that—with Danica Keyes was complicated. Most people didn't know it existed. Julep wasn't even certain herself if it was real. All she knew was that she didn't know what to expect when it came to the most popular girl in the sixth grade. There was the Danica who came to Julep's rescue when she needed a hand opening her sticky locker; who complimented Julep on her writing; who cared when Julep had thrown up her egg-salad sandwich all over the gym floor. Yet there was also the Danica who laughed at Julep's audition when the goslings were around; who deliberately yawned eight times during Julep's oral report in science when the goslings were around; who pretended Julep didn't exist when the goslings were around (there did seem to be a distinct connection between Danica's treatment of her and the precise location of the goslings).

Julep felt like one of the many gold charms clinging to the eighteen-karat-gold bracelet on Danica's wrist. There was a horse, a high-heeled shoe, a basket of flowers, an outline of a heart, a cross, and a few others Julep had never gotten close enough to identify. But she certainly could relate to their predicament. For Julep was on the gold chain, too; a human-girl charm, hanging on that bracelet day after day. Now and then Danica glanced at her. Usually, though, she didn't. Julep wasn't looking to be part of Danica's inner circle. She had her own friends. Good ones. Better ones. She only wanted Danica to make a decision. Julep wanted to know where they stood once and for all.

Laying her cheek in her palm, Julep watched Betsy hold out another licorice rope. The Head Goose wrapped her fingers around it. A small gift between friends was hardly worth noting, unless you knew a little more than you were supposed to about everyone involved. And Julep did. She couldn't help thinking that a lot of acting sure went on in middle school. Very little of it onstage.

6 Guaranteed to Work, or Your Money Back

Y ou want me to tell Mrs. Picklehaupt *what*?"

"You're going to be a tutor at Valley View."

"She'll never go for it."

It was common knowledge that only the most trusted honor students were selected to be reading, writing, and math tutors for the elementary grades. Why, even the More Girl didn't make the cut this year. In all fairness, only two of the twelve kids chosen as tutors were from the sixth grade. It was a popular job. Not only did you earn credit but every once in a while you got to work at Valley View during the day and skip a class or two. Supreme sweetness!

Trig followed Julep down the stairs on their way to third period to explain. "Tell Mrs. Picklehaupt you signed up for it before you tried out for the play. Say you found out a few days ago they are shorthanded. Say they desperately need you. That you'll be helping a kid learn to write—oh—I've got it! You're going to tutor a little orphan girl, you know, one without parents—"

"That's usually what *orphan* means."

"Yeah, and she has . . . uh . . . really bad eyesight, so she has to wear these gigantic glasses. What is it when you can only see far away but not close up?"

"Farsighted."

"That's it. And she should be sick—"

"Don't you think you've done enough to her?"

"Nothing too awful . . . um . . . how about the chicken pox? Yeah, the chicken pox." Trig grinned at his own genius. "You're helping an orphan with bad eyesight and the chicken pox learn to write. It's a surefire excuse. With a story like that, Mrs. Picklehaupt couldn't possibly guilt you into staying."

Julep pushed her bangs out of her eyes. "Is that the best you've got?"

Trig gave her a wounded look. "Well, you could always say you're volunteering at my uncle's spay and neuter clinic for ferrets, but it'll only buy you a few days. I've tried it before. I don't know why, but teachers don't feel that sorry for un-neutered weasels." With a parting wave, Trig peeled off to go to the social-studies wing. "Use the tutoring one. Guaranteed to work or your money back."

Julep sputtered air between her lips. Farsighted orphans or neutered ferrets. She had expected better from Trig Maxwell.

After school, Julep joined the crowd of kids clustered around Mrs. Picklehaupt. Tessa needed the drama teacher's approval on a purchase order. Kathleen, it turned out, required more fabric to finish the mattress covers (what a shocker!). Betsy couldn't wait to inform Mrs. Picklehaupt, and everyone else within a ten-mile radius, that she would be the lucky one to say the new line (Jillian was nowhere to be found). As their teacher handled one question, problem, and minicrisis after another, the group of students dwindled. Julep hung back. She wanted to be last so no one would hear what she was about to say.

Oh, crêpe suzettes! What *was* she about to say?

Julep's heart began to race and she was losing the feeling in the tips of her fingers. She couldn't remember a single thing Trig had told her.

Relax. Take a breath. Not like you're going underwater to break a Guinness world record!

As the feeling returned to her hands, so did the details of Trig's "surefire excuse."

Tutor. Orphan girl. Big glasses. And what was the other thing?

Tutor. Orphan girl. Big glasses. And . . .

". . . all actors onstage now. Let's go." A pair of clapping hands brought Julep back to reality.

"Mrs. Picklehaupt?" Julep burst. "I need to—"

"A moment, dear." A pointy chin with one very noticeable black whisker turned toward the stage. "A reminder, people, we are off-script today."

A nervous murmur went through the cast.

"Cherry Anne, while I run to the restroom would you please round up the—" Peeking over her turquoise fiberglass clipboard, Mrs. Picklehaupt scoured the cafeteria. "Where's my narrator? Where's Cherry Anne?"

Millie poked her head out from behind the red velvet curtain. "She said something about an audition for a soup commercial." She frowned. "Or was it soap? I forgot. But she has to go to the Community Playhouse afterward, so she won't be back today."

The drama teacher sighed heavily and rubbed the back of her neck. After a moment, a stick-figure body swung around. Two gray marble eyes locked onto Julep. "Tulip, dear, would you mind collecting all the scripts from the actors?"

"Me?"

She nodded, and tar-black hair, the strands thinner than angel-hair spaghetti, brushed against her shoulder.

"I guess so, but—"

"Thank you, Tulip."

"It's, uh . . . actually, Julep. My name, I . . . I . . . mean," she stammered to the back of an olive turtleneck that was already leaving the room.

Somewhat bewildered, Julep began gathering scripts.

"I knew my singing partner wouldn't abandon me," Bernadette said, handing over her pages. Julep didn't have the heart to tell her co-best friend that she wouldn't be here much longer. Deep in hushed conversation, Betsy and Jillian tossed their scripts into Julep's arms with barely a glance at her. Danica Keyes, on the other hand, watched Julep's every move with worried green eyes. Julep grasped one end of a wrinkled page that had started to tear under the pressure of Danica's fingers. "Script, please," she said.

"Uh-huh. Uh-huh." Danica's rapid nodding reminded Julep of one of those bobblehead dolls. Still, white knuckles did not release their grip.

Julep didn't understand why Danica was so frazzled. She had nothing to be concerned about. Popular people rarely embarrassed themselves or were embarrassed by others, which, now that she thought about it, probably had a lot to do with *why* they were so popular. After a minor tussle, Danica finally parted with her script.

Julep had to go up onstage to get Calvin's script. He and Eddie were pretending to be contestants in a bodybuilding competition, striking ridiculous poses and flexing their acorn-size biceps. Calvin stopped his Mr. Universe performance long enough to get his script out of his notebook. However, when Julep reached for it, Calvin whipped it away. He held it out again. Before her fingers could latch on to it, he yanked it away once more.

"Calvin," Julep warned.

"What? You're the one not taking it." Narrowing his fiendish eyes, Calvin raised his right arm straight up over his head. He was three inches taller than Julep, and that long, scrawny arm of his put the pages completely out of her grasp.

Chomping on his gum, Calvin blew a bright green bubble. He popped it in her face. "Don't you want it?" He did a little jig around her. "What are you waiting for O'Fool? Come and get it."

Julep hated when he called her that. Calvin wanted her to jump so he could make her look silly. She had no intention of bouncing around like a crazed poodle going after a rubber toy. But what could she do? People were starting to stare. People were starting to laugh. Calvin stuck his left arm up, too, clasping his left hand around his right wrist to support it.

As he circled her, kicking his feet out, a thought crossed Julep's mind. If she couldn't get to the script, then the next logical move would be to get the script to come to her, right? Julep carefully set her pile on the floor. She moved toward Calvin. He stopped doing his Irish dance so he could focus on keeping his arms in the air. It was exactly what she'd counted on. Calvin was looking up, eagerly anticipating her first frenetic leap into the air. But Julep didn't leave the floor. Instead, she put one hand on each side of his ribs and began to tickle him. Five seconds later, Calvin dropped his script, along with a big wad of sour-apple gum.

"Mission accomplished." Julep scurried to retrieve the pages. "Maybe next time you'll cooperate when I ask nicely."

Yeah. Right. Insert snort here.

Once Julep rounded up the scripts, she stacked all of them but one in a cardboard box marked SCRIPTS sitting on an end table. The other she placed on Mrs. Picklehaupt's folding chair. Her task complete, Julep considered walking out without saying anything more to anyone. But she didn't.

"Did you get every one of them?" The drama teacher was coming her way.

"Yes, Mrs. Picklehaupt."

"Please put them in the box marked—oh"—she glanced down—"you've done it already. Smart girl." She bent to get a script.

"I also put one on your chair."

The little whisker on her chin stood at attention. "Very smart girl."

Julep beamed. She couldn't recall anyone ever calling her smart. Let alone very smart. Even so . . .

You know what you have to do. Get it over as quickly as possible. Tutor. Orphan girl. Big glasses. And . . .

Why couldn't she remember that last one?

Mrs. Picklehaupt was instructing the cast to begin after Cherry Anne's opening introduction.

"Here." The drama teacher thrust a script at Julep. "You can be my prompter."

"Huh?"

"Whenever someone gets stuck on a line, you prompt them. That means you read the line out loud to them. Think you can handle it, Tulip?"

"Well, I—"

"Line!" shouted Danica.

Soon, Julep was so busy feeding the actors their lines she didn't have time to think about quitting. By the end of rehearsal, only Bernadette had gotten through her part without help from Julep. Most of the actors came off the stage looking worn and frustrated and ready to smack one another. Mrs. Picklehaupt said that was normal. She said they would get better. Julep certainly hoped so because they were pretty awful. She circulated the cardboard box so people could take back their scripts.

"Don't get too attached," said their drama teacher. "Another week and you'll be off-script for good."

Danica dropped her pages. They landed at Julep's feet. The Head Goose quickly retrieved them. She straightened and swung to go, then suddenly turned back. Danica glanced down at Julep's black ballet-style shoes with the embroidered hearts. Three tiny furrows etched their way across her forehead. But she didn't say anything. Neither did Julep. The next thing Julep knew, Danica was being swept out the door by her goslings.

By the time Julep returned the empty script box to Mrs. Picklehaupt, the cafeteria had almost cleared out. Trig and Bernadette stood at the back door, waiting for her.

"Tessa says you're doing a great job on the sets." Mrs. Picklehaupt took the box from Julep. "I've seen your papier-mâché work. It's wonderful."

Julep shuddered. No way was she was going back to *that*. "Thanks, but see, I have this other thing . . . a tutoring thing, I mean. And it's over at the elementary school . . . and they really need me there so . . . you know, to help kids . . . at the elementary school. Did I say that already?"

It's a surefire excuse, remember? Stick to the basics.

Tutor. Orphan girl. Big glasses. And . . . and . . . WHAT?

"That's nice. I think," said Mrs. Picklehaupt, scrunching up her lips. "Anyway, you've been an excellent assistant director today . . ."

Assistant director?

". . . and I could certainly use a self-starter like you to give me a hand on a regular basis, if you're interested."

Mrs. Picklehaupt called me a self-starter. How about that? I'm a self-starter.

What did that mean, exactly?

"So what do you think, Tulip?"

Julep slapped a palm to her forehead. "Chicken pox!"

That was the thing! Tutor. Orphan girl. Big glasses. *Chicken pox.*

Marble eyes were gazing at her, puzzled.

"I mean, Julep," she corrected, her face catching fire. "My name isn't Tulip. It's Julep."

"Oh, I am so sorry, dear." The drama teacher stuck her head through the hole in her black crocheted poncho. "See you tomorrow, then?"

Julep's fingers closed around the straps on her backpack. Should she agree to do it? A half hour ago she was dead set against ever coming back here again. Stage crew had been a colossal disaster. But assistant director—that *did* sounded promising.

"Before I forget, Julep." Mrs. Picklehaupt made a point to emphasize the *J* in her name. "Way to handle Calvin."

Julep slung her backpack over one shoulder. She smiled. "See you tomorrow, Mrs. Picklehaupt."

7 Knowing It By Heart

8:21 P.M.   Mood: Psyched!

Dear Amelia:

I've been A.D. (yes, me!) for six whole days and my life is A.I.F! Can you process it? One minute I'm gluing tissue paper to myself and the next I'm second in command! And to think I was seconds away from quitting.

Mrs. Picklehaupt is teaching me about stage direction. For instance, stage left is to the actor's left when he's standing on

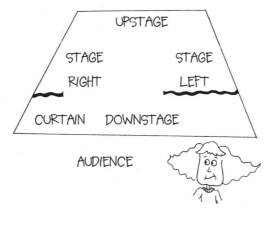

UPSTAGE

STAGE RIGHT   STAGE LEFT

CURTAIN   DOWNSTAGE

AUDIENCE

the stage facing the audience, which would be my right when I'm sitting next to Mrs. P. looking at the stage. Get it? Don't feel bad if you're lost. It's confusing.

Sometimes, Mrs. P. has me take an actor into the hallway to "run lines." I read all the other roles in the script so the person can work to memorize their part. I'm not supposed to talk about who is the worst at learning lines, but her initials are D.K.! ☺

The best thing about being A.D. is that Mrs. Picklehaupt listens to me. Sometimes, she even uses my ideas, like the one about having the princess carry a wet, inside-out umbrella into the castle when she comes in from the storm. That was MY idea. Cool, huh?

Bernadette says I am a natural A.D. Isn't she the B.F.P.?

C.Y.L.,

Julep Antoinette O'Toole, Assistant Director

Julep's Decoder Page
KEEP OUT!   PERSONAL STUFF!

A.D.:   Assistant Director (what else?)

A.I.F.:   Amazing, Incredible, and Fantastic!

D.K.:   I promised Mrs. Picklehaupt to keep it a secret so

you'll have to figure this one out on your own. Big hint:
$200 jeans!

B.F.P.:   Best Friend on the Planet

MAY ANYONE WHO READS THIS GET
DANDRUFF THE SIZE OF SNOWFLAKES!

"How did you sleep, Princess?"

"Poorly. Very poorly, indeed. I . . . uh . . . ummmmm . . . wait a sec, Julep, don't tell me. I know this . . . we just did this . . . oh, yeah . . . Why, I hardly closed my eyes all might, I mean, all *night*."

Sitting on the checkerboard floor, her back to the wall, Julep looked up from the page. "What if you yawned after you said 'very poorly, indeed'? You could stretch your arms up, you know, for effect."

"I like that." Danica knelt beside Julep and took her script back.

While she made the notation in the margin, Julep peered down the empty hallway outside the cafeteria. She wished someone—anyone—would walk by right now. When you're running lines after school with the most popular girl in the sixth grade, you really should have a witness. Or a camera. Preferably a witness *with* a camera. A janitor did not count, which was too bad because Mr. Havlett was the only one around. He was rolling a mop and bucket toward the boys' bathroom.

Popping the yellow top onto her gel pen, Danica handed her

script back to Julep. She stood up, straightening a new white miniskirt with a tie-dyed fuchsia belt. Danica used both hands to flip her long hair over her shoulders. Her black velvet locks stood out against a crisp white long-sleeved tee. So many times Julep had wished for shiny, sleek, waist-length hair that ended in dozens of cute corkscrew curls, instead of her own mass of wild brush-breaking waves.

"I'll start again," said Danica. "Poorly. Very poorly, indeed." She yawned, patting her mouth with one hand. She puffed out her chest and lifted her elbows in a good stretch. Julep silently congratulated herself. She was certain Mrs. Picklehaupt would approve, too, once she saw how realistic the move was.

Danica kept going. "Why, I hardly closed my eyes all night."

Julep read the next line, which was Bernadette's. "Whatever was the matter?"

"I don't know exactly, but there was . . . there was . . ."—she fought to reach the next word—"uh . . . something hard under all those mattresses and feather beds, I'm certain of it." Danica slowly rubbed her thumb against a heart-shaped jaw. She fingered one of her curls. She twirled her charm bracelet around her wrist. After fifteen seconds of agony, Danica yelled, "Line!"

"All night it—"

"All night it kept poking me. I'm black-and-blue all over. Look at me, I . . . uh . . . uh . . . I have bruises from the top of my royal head to the very tips of my royal toes. Or is it shoes?"

"Toes."

"Right—to the tips of my royal toes."

"What was it?"

"I'm not sure. I only know it was quite hard. It might have been a brick."

"Perhaps it was."

"Yet, it was round, too. It might have been a seashell."

"Perhaps it was."

"It was also very large. It might have been a . . . a . . . oh, I knew I'd forget the last one." Danica squished her lips up one cheek. She pushed her sleeves up to her elbows. She nearly pulled the tiny, gold high-heeled shoe off her bracelet, before wailing, "This is impossible, Julep. I can't think of it."

"Yes, you can." Julep concentrated on the line, trying to send it to Danica with her mind. *It might have been a boulder. Boulder. Say "boulder."* Julep closed her eyes. *Come on, Danica, we've gone over this three times. You know this!*

"I *don't* know it," came the eerie answer. "All I can think of is a bowling ball, and that's not right."

"But it is a lot a funnier than a boulder."

"Boulder!" She slapped her pen against her thigh. "Boulder! I knew it. This is never going to work. As soon as I remember one line, I forget the—"

Next to Julep's head, the *chu-chunk* of the cafeteria door cut her off. Tessa Galloway appeared from behind it to say, "Julep, Mrs. Picklehaupt needs you." She went back inside.

Julep stood up and held Danica's script out to her.

"You can't leave yet," protested the Head Goose. "We haven't even gotten to my big speech on page twenty—"

"Don't worry," said Julep, twisting to brush off the back of her jeans. "I'll find someone else to prompt you."

"I don't want anyone else."

Her hands on her rear, Julep froze.

Hello? Did the most popular girl in the sixth grade just announce she didn't want anybody but Julep Antoinette O'Toole, Assistant Director, to run lines with her? Could we have an instant replay here because I think she did! And where, oh, WHERE is everybody when you need them?

"Okay," said Julep, her body flooding with happiness. "Let me see what Mrs. Picklehaupt wants and I'll be right back."

"Promise?" Danica flapped her hands rapidly as if her silver fingernails were wet.

Julep pulled on the cafeteria door. It was all she could do to keep her feet on the ground. "Promise."

Were all actors this needy? Julep hoped so. She didn't have to dive very far into her imagination to visualize what it could mean for her future.

Holding her trusty clipboard, Julep leans on the arm of her chair—the one with her name printed on the back panel in hot pink cursive letters (the perfect color for the hottest new director in Hollywood). Leonardo DiCaprio has demanded that she direct his next film. And Julep, of course, has agreed. While sitting in her cushy director's chair, Julep snacks on peanut-butter crackers and chocolate milk (delivered on a silver tray by her sister). "Oh, Julep, you're the best director in the world," Leonardo says, his piercing blue (or is it green?) eyes gazing into hers. [Note: check the official Leonardo DiCaprio Web site for correct eye color.] Delicately, Julep licks the peanut butter from her fingers, looks deep into Leonardo's blue/green eyes, and says, "I know." When you're a brilliant director, everyone trusts you. Everyone believes in you. And nothing, absolutely noth-ing, ever goes wrong.

"Could you go down to the copy room?" Mrs. Picklehaupt was asking Julep. "Jillian is missing a couple of pages from her script."

"Nine pages," muttered Jillian.

"Nine?" The drama teacher's eyebrows shot up.

Julep noticed that Mrs. Picklehaupt looked different today. Her face had a grayish-green tinge and she seemed thinner, if that was possible.

"I need page two, twelve, fifteen . . . uh, let's see . . ." Jillian thumbed through her script, "twenty-six, and thirty through thirty-four."

Julep scribbled the page numbers on the palm of her hand with her ballpoint pen. She picked up Mrs. Picklehaupt's script to make the copies. On her way out, she passed three people: Calvin, who burped at her, Eddie, who tried to burp but couldn't get any noise to come out, and Betsy, who was sitting at a table digging through her steel-gray backpack.

"I don't know what happened," Jillian was saying to Mrs. Picklehaupt behind her.

Julep's legs slowed.

"That's not why I'm upset," replied their drama teacher. "Your part is not that large, Jillian. You should be off-script by now."

As a hand dug around inside a gray designer backpack, two lips covered in apple-pie-à-la-mode lip balm turned up ever so slightly at the corners. The smirk quickly vanished. But not quickly enough. Someone had seen it. Julep had seen it. She'd

expected as much from Betsy. What she didn't expect, however, was for Gosling Number One to suddenly grab her pack,
jump up, and trail Julep into the hall.

"I'm glad that didn't take too—" Danica's voice dried up the
moment Betsy stepped out of Julep's shadow.

"Aloha," called Betsy. It was her not-so-subtle way of re-
minding everyone that her family had a time-share condo in
Hawaii. Big woo.

Although Danica replied with a simple, "Hey," a chill skidded down Julep's arms. It was as if the temperature in the hallway had suddenly dropped fifty degrees. A thin sheet of ice
was already glazing over Danica's pretty green eyes.

Julep tried to crack it. "I have to go to the office, but we can
run lines when I get back," she said.

The wintry eyes peered through her.

"You dropped—" Julep started to tell Danica that the top to
her gel pen was on the floor, but Betsy never gave her the
chance.

"Mrs. Picklehaupt is in a crummy mood." Betsy had an arm
around Danica's shoulders, spinning her away from Julep. "You
should have heard her lay into Jillian. I felt so bad for her. I
mean, she's not a very good actress and now she can't even
keep track of her script." Betsy glanced over her shoulder, narrowing her eyes at Julep. "Don't you have something to do?"

"I . . . I . . . I . . ." The cogs in her brain stuck fast, Julep
whirled around and sped down the hallway as fast as she could
without actually running (there was a rule against that). Why is

it that whenever one of the popular girls spoke to her, Julep ended up sounding like a hungry seagull?

She made Jillian's copies in less than five minutes. Tucking the pages under her arm, Julep took off for the cafeteria (again walking as fast as she could without breaking into a jog). She zipped down the main hallway and cut through the courtyard outside the science wing. Julep hurried through the red metal door, trotted down the short entry hall, and turned left. "Hey, Danica, I'm . . ." Julep's rubber soles braked. ". . . alone."

The hallway outside the cafeteria was empty, but for the top of Danica's yellow gel pen, still lying on a white tile.

Julep had been too slow.

Who was she kidding? Two seconds in the copy room wouldn't have been fast enough. She had thought, well, hoped, that being assistant director might change the way Danica viewed her. It had been working, too. The two of them were on the edge of something. Julep had felt it. If only Betsy hadn't barged in and ruined everything.

It's not all Betsy's fault. Danica could have waited for you, if she'd wanted.

She could do a lot of things if she wanted.

With a will of their own, Julep's Follicles of Fury, as Trig called them, began to tingle. Julep scratched her scalp above her ear. Head up, eyes straight, she set her jaw. Deliberately, she chose her path to the cafeteria door, feeling the satisfying crunch of plastic under her foot.

8 Plan Number Three

Wearing a pair of rainbow-trout oven mitts, Julep's mother set a steaming rectangle on the dining-room table. "I hope you're in the mood for pumpkin bake," she said, brushing a strand of reddish-brown hair away from her face with one of the big fish mitts.

"Look, everybody," said Julep with a broad grin, "a burnt-orange casserole in a burnt-orange casserole dish."

From the opposite end of the table Julep's dad grinned, though he tried to hide it. To her right, Harmony and Kyle both chuckled. Cooper, sitting on Julep's left, laughed the hardest. Her mom, however, didn't change expression. Obviously, she had not found Julep's remark at all amusing. Julep thought it was clever. After all, they *did* match. It wasn't her fault her mother had cooked the pumpkin bake too long, leaving everything but the center singed and rock-hard.

"Kyle?" Julep's mother held out her hand to their guest. A slight frown creasing his forehead, he handed over his plate.

Kyle Patterson was Harmony's first real boyfriend, though the two were not allowed to go out on a date—not until Harmony was sixteen. It was not something Julep's sister had willingly agreed to. "You're killing my social life," she whined to their parents almost every Friday night. Julep didn't see why her sister got worked up over boys. They were SO not worth it.

Ninety-nine percent of the boys at Heatherwood Middle School were loud, rude, and immature. And they smelled. Plenty of times Julep had been forced to sit downwind from a guy fresh out of P.E. class (Mr. Hogan didn't enforce the showering rule for boys the way Mrs. Springborg, a.k.a. The Borg, did with the girls). Whew! What was it going to take to clue boys in to a modern thing called deodorant?

With the no-dating-until-you're-sixteen rule in effect, the best Harmony could do was invite Kyle for dinner or to do homework. Julep's mother was now chiseling out a burned corner of squiggly noodles, dotted with chickpeas, onions, and red peppers, held together by gooey pumpkin strings and soy cheese. Someone should have warned Kyle that all of the O'Toole women had a defective cooking gene. The casserole hit his plate with a *plonk*.

When Julep's mom went for a crystal bowl filled with toasted pumpkin seeds, Kyle rushed to say, "Oh, no thanks."

"No seeds?" Mrs. O'Toole looked hurt.

"Maybe a few."

"I want seeds on mine," said Cooper. "Lots of 'em, Mom." Cooper was supposed to wait until they'd said grace before eating, but Julep saw him sneak a pumpkin seed off his plate.

Shifting in her straight-backed chair, Julep waited for her mother to fill her plate, too. It was strange being here. Her family rarely used their formal dining room, unless they had company. She wondered why they couldn't eat in here when nobody special was coming over. Seemed like a real waste of gold-leaf wallpaper, silk curtains, and a fake orange tree to her.

Once everyone had pumpkin bake on their plate, they passed around the spinach salad, cracked-wheat rolls, and stuffed tomatoes. Julep's father led them in saying grace, and then it was time to dig in and eat. Julep pulled her big lemon-and-lime-striped cardigan tighter around her, fluffing out the two big side pockets.

"Mom," she said, trying to cut into her crispy pumpkin cube. It resisted. "Mrs. Picklehaupt liked my idea about having Danica wear flannel jammies with the feet in them."

"Did you tell her about the old-fashioned ruffled cap?"

"Yep. We're going to do it, too."

"Terrific." Her mother turned to glance at Kyle. "Julep's the assistant director of the play at Heatherwood."

Julep sat up taller. "You want to come to my play, Kyle?"

Kyle said he would. Harmony rolled her eyes to indicate she had no intention of taking her boyfriend to her annoying little sister's lame-o play; especially when that annoying little sister didn't even have a speaking part.

After watching Kyle prod his tomato a few times, Julep said softly, "They're filled with leeks."

"Really?" He inspected it again. "Mine's not."

"Sure it is. They all are."

"How do you know?"

"I made them."

"You did?" Kyle shook his thick, curly hair. "On purpose?"

"Uh-huh." She began buttering her roll.

"Why would you poke holes in all the tomatoes?"

Julep gave him an odd look. "I didn't."

"But you just said you did."

"No, I didn't."

"You said they were leaking."

Julep threw her head back and let out a squeal. "No, I said they were filled with leeks."

"And I'm telling you mine is perfectly fine." Kyle was starting to get irritated. He flipped his tomato on its side to show her that the bottom was intact. "See?"

Julep tried to explain that she had meant *leek,* as in the vegetable, not *leak,* as in the hole, but was laughing too hard. Her parents and Cooper started snickering, too. Kyle looked confused. Harmony looked liked she wanted to stab someone, mainly Julep, with her butter knife. Clutching her achy stomach, Julep finally was able to say, "Not *l-e-a-k. L-e-e-k.* A leek is like an onion."

Kyle's face turned the same shade as his stuffed tomato.

Still giggling, Julep said, "In band today, Miss Crosetti read us a cool news story. It was all about some musicians in Germany who make musical instruments out of vegetables."

Her dad did a double take. "Vegetables?"

"The orchestra members actually carve their own instruments. They make flutes from carrots and saxophones out of cucumbers—"

"Kyle plays drums in the marching band," interjected Harmony, giving Julep a vicious glare.

"I want to play drums," shot Cooper.

"No, you don't," their parents said simultaneously.

"Anyway," said Julep, shooting her sister a return stare that was just as frigid, "once the instruments are done, they tune them, and play a concert. Then after the concert—"

"You're making this up," snapped Harmony.

"Am not. Anyway, when they're done with the concert, guess what they do?"

Nobody knew.

"They chop up their instruments and make soup!"

They all howled, except her sister. It was hard to tell if it was because Harmony didn't think it was funny or because she'd just taken a bite of burnt-orange casserole. Probably both.

"That certainly brings a whole new meaning to the term *musical fruit*," said Julep's dad, prompting Cooper to wave his fork like a bandleader's baton and begin chanting, "Beans, beans, the musical fruit—"

"Cooper, stop!" cried Harmony.

Their brother, of course, only upped the volume. "The more you eat the more you toot. The more you toot the better you feel, so eat your beans at e-ver-y meal. Wa-hoo!" By the time Cooper had finished his song, Harmony had surrendered— literally. She was waving her white napkin at their mother.

Julep, meanwhile, had taken the opportunity to inch her pumpkin bake toward the rim of her plate. The timing for Plan Number Three was critical. It was important that no one, particularly a parent, see how her chunk of charred casserole left this world. Julep wriggled the fingers of her right hand, warming them up. If this was to work, every element of the plan would have to be seamless, swift, and, above all, stealthy. The block of casserole teetering on the edge of her plate and her plate close to the edge of the table, Julep waited. She waited through discussions of favorite vacation spots and high-school football and weird sandwiches. She waited through her dad's lecture on why the Beatles were *the* best band ever (like she needed to hear that again). Finally, Kyle asked, "May I have another roll, please?" And P.N.T. was off and running.

Julep's mother handed the wicker breadbasket to Cooper. Cooper gave it to Julep, who took it with her left hand. She moved the basket slowly across the plate, a.k.a. the target area. However, before she passed it to Kyle, Julep dipped it over the center of the target area. Using the bottom of the basket, she firmly tapped her piece of casserole. *Plop!* The hunk fell easily into her cupped right hand hovering a few inches below the tabletop. While her left hand made sure the basket smoothly continued on its way, her hand effortlessly dumped the pumpkin bake into the pocket of her lemon-lime cardigan. As all of this was happening, Julep did not change expression. She did not even look down. What technique! What precision! She had executed P.N.T. flawlessly.

Everyone kept right on talking and eating. They had seen nothing. Of course, it hadn't always been this way. More than a few times the food had landed in her lap, on the floor, or tragically, on someone else. But today's exercise was sheer perfection, if she did say so herself. It was a masterful performance of finely honed skill balanced with a—

"I saw that," hissed Kyle, looking down at her bulging pocket.

Julep froze! Her cover was blown. Harmony's boyfriend was going to bust her now, for sure. Her sister was certainly going to get a jolt and a half out of seeing Julep get in mega-trouble.

Kyle was crooking his finger at her. "How," he whispered, "*did* you do that?"

Julep relaxed. He didn't want to spill her secret. He wanted to repeat it!

"Got pockets?"

Kyle tugged on the front muff of his Snohomish High School sweatshirt. "Just this."

"It'll do."

A half hour later, the two of them were running down the path to the woods behind Julep's house. Julep scampered up onto the flat granite rock overlooking the pond. She held her shriveled chunk of casserole in one hand and placed the other hand on her heart. "We salute you, O pumpkin, for giving your life for such a horrible casserole."

Kyle was staring up at her. "Now what?"

"We throw it in. And pray it sinks."

"Can I chuck it any way I want?"

"Uh-huh." She cocked her arm. "But I like to aim for the middle. It's the deepest part. There's less chance it will resurface there."

"Are you sure it's okay? I mean, is this stuff good for wildlife?"

Julep had never considered that before. Come to think of it, Cooper had recently complained he wasn't catching as many minnows as he used to.

Peering through the cattails, Julep sighed. "The way I figure it, it's either them or us."

Kyle glanced down at the scorched pumpkin bake in his hand. They looked at each other.

"Us."

11:03 P.M.   Mood: Bouncy

Dear Amelia:

I am still awake. Nothing is wrong. Actually, everything is right. That's the problem. Life is too right to waste it sleeping!

Harmony's boyfriend, Kyle, came for dinner tonight. My mom ~~cooked~~ burned her famous pumpkin bake. Gag-o-matic! I know it's forbidden, but I had to let Kyle in on P.N.T. He swore to keep it T.S.F.E! Now I know why he's the pitcher on his baseball team. Good arm! Kyle's fun, which burns me 'cause I may have to rethink my theory that 99 percent of the male species are dingleberries. Of course, he could be in that one percent of non-dingleberry boys, like Trig.

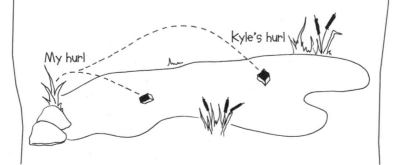

My hurl

Kyle's hurl

Tomorrow, at play rehearsal we are going to start assembling the set. I L.L.L. being assistant director. After ice skating, ballet dancing, chorus, piano, and Campfire Girls (remember the H.F?), it's great to FINALLY get something right.

Good night, sleep tight, and don't let the pumpkin bake bite!

C.Y.L.,

Julep, A.D.

Julep's Decoder Page

VAMOOSE!　　GET LOST!

T.S.F.E.: Top Secret For Eternity

P.N.T.: Plan Number Three

L.L.L.: LOVE, LOVE, LOVE!

H.F.: Hair Fire (warning: if you have BIG wavy hair, do not bend down to blow on a fire to keep it going).

WHAT PART OF SCRAM DON'T YOU UNDERSTAND?

9 The End (Already?)

Julep struggled to pry apart the metal snaps on her olive-green raincoat. One of Harmony's recent hand-me-downs, it was, as usual, too big for her. In it, she felt like one of those ten person camping tents. Firmly gripping both sides of the vinyl lapel, Julep pulled and grunted. The snaps didn't budge. She tried again, glad that no one was in the hallway to catch the wrestling match live.

"Hey," said Danica, resting her dark head against the bank of lockers.

A clap of thunder shook the building. With one brutal yank, the snaps came loose.

Danica ran a finger along the edge of Julep's locker door. "It's not sticking anymore."

"Not today," said Julep, slightly out of breath. She shook the coat from her shoulders. "Come back tomorrow. It likes to surprise me."

Lightning flashed in the window behind Danica, creating a white halo around her head. "You're here early."

"My mom dropped me off on her way to work."

"Mine, too. I hate storms."

"I love them."

Thunder rumbled. Danica played with the hollow heart hanging from her charm bracelet.

"I have to go," Julep said, trying to stuff the vinyl coat into the bottom of her locker. It barely fit. She wasn't in the mood to play Danica's game of *Are We Friends Today or Not?* Besides, she *did* have to go. Trig was getting a ride to school as well, and the two of them were planning to meet at the second-story drinking fountain.

"I like your sweater."

"This?" Julep checked out her faded, cream sweater with the missing middle button and the hem that was unraveling. Was Danica serious? Or was she up to something? Julep tugged on one of the frayed puffball ties of her very comfy, but very ugly sweater. "It's not new."

"It's still nice."

Up to something.

Julep reached for her math textbook and notebook. "I have to go," she said again.

"Do you think we'll have drama club after school?"

"They only call baseball on account of rain, not plays."

"We can run lines again."

"I . . . I . . . don't think so."

Whew! One squawk away from becoming a seagull again.

Danica licked her lips. "Is it because I didn't wait for you last week?"

Julep pretended to search her locker for something. She didn't want to answer that.

"I wanted to stay," said Danica, "but Betsy needed—"

A snort cut her off.

Oh, gosh! Did that come from me?

"Julep! Why are you being so weird?"

"Me? Weird? Ha!"

Okay, that *was* weird.

Julep looked at her watch. "Are you sure you should be standing here talking to me? Someone could come down the hall any second and see us."

"What do you—?"

Julep shut her locker door. "I have to meet Trig."

"But what about this afternoon? Who's going to help me learn my lines?"

"Ask one of the gos—I mean, Betsy. She thinks you're great." Julep stalked away. Feeling a little stronger, a little bolder, she threw one last remark over her shoulder. "At least, to your face." She didn't look back. She wasn't *that* bold.

When Julep reached the end of the hall, she turned into the stairwell. A quick glance to the left her told her that Danica was gone. She felt a twinge of guilt. But it couldn't be helped. Hugging her books to her chest, Julep took the steps two at a time. She had been dangling from Danica Keyes's charm bracelet long enough. It was time to break free.

Wah-ahh-aaaaawk.

Julep fought to hold the note for all four beats in the measure, but her lungs gave out. With a dwindling supply of air flowing through the trumpet, the note sputtered and faded away until, sadly, the D died on the practice room floor. Had he been there, Trig would have taken off his cap, said a prayer, and buried it.

Julep lowered her trumpet and steadied the bell on the knee of her jeans. She wiped her sore lips on the back of her hand. Waiting for her music teacher's comments, she couldn't raise her head to meet his eyes. Mr. Dellabalma did not speak. Instead, he stroked his short black goatee and paced slowly around the tiny room in a figure eight. Julep pressed down on the valves of her trumpet, silently going over her fingering again. She had made a lot of mistakes. But it wasn't her fault. She had been so busy with the play she'd barely had time to take her trumpet out of its case lately. Julep readjusted her mouthpiece, being careful not to push it in too hard. Once, just after she'd gotten it, she had pounded it into place with the heel of her boot. It had gotten stuck. Her dad had to take it down to Mill Creek Music so the technician could remove the mouthpiece without damaging it or the instrument.

Mr. Dellabalma stopped in front of Julep's music stand. "Are you happy with that?"

"No," she said hoarsely.

"You're puffing out your cheeks again."

"Sorry."

"And overtightening your embouchure to reach the F."

She dropped her head. "Sorry."

"By now, you should be able to hold that D for four counts." Julep stroked a puffball tie. "Sorry."

"I thought you wanted to move up at the next challenge."

"I do."

Her concert-band teacher, Miss Crosetti, arranged each of the sections—clarinets, saxophones, flutes, etc.—from the best to worst students. She didn't use those words, of course. She said "more skilled players" and "less skilled players," but who was she kidding? Everybody knew the person who sat in the first chair was the best musician in the group and the person who sat in the last chair was the worst. The top few players got the most difficult parts to play, including the solos. The most pathetic players got stuck with the dullest parts and no solos at all. The only time you could move up the line of chairs in your section was during a Chair Challenge, which happened every three weeks or so. That's when those in the lower chairs got to pick someone in an upper chair to "challenge." You each played the same song for Miss Crosetti and she decided if the challenger was good enough to beat the challengee, and take his/her chair. Of course, you never wanted to take on someone whom you knew could beat you, which was why Julep had yet to challenge anyone. She'd only been in concert band for three months.

Bernadette was first-chair oboe. Okay, she was the *only* chair. But she was so good that she also played with the eighth-grade symphonic band. Julep was seventh-chair trumpet. The downside was that there were only seven trumpet players in band. The upside was that Julep didn't have to worry about anybody challenging for her chair. At first, nobody thought much of her being in seventh chair because she was the newest trumpet player. But now, after four challenges, they were starting to notice she had yet to move up. Eddie Levitt, who was in

77

sixth chair, made fun of the fact that she was one of the "less skilled players." Though he didn't say it like that. "You're the rear end of the trumpet section, Julep" is how he said it. "That's a good spot for you 'cause when you play you sound like a farting elephant."

"I *do* want to move up, Mr. Dellabalma," insisted Julep, shutting Eddie's words out of her mind.

"You'll have to practice an hour a day."

"*Every* day?"

"You get out of it what you put into it, Julep."

She hated clichéd sayings like that. It seemed to Julep she was putting an awful lot into the trumpet, and not getting much out of it.

After her lesson, Julep zipped across campus to the cafeteria. Mrs. Picklehaupt had given her permission to show up late for play rehearsal on lesson days. As she sped, Julep vowed to become a more dedicated musician. An hour a day wasn't so bad, especially if it meant you got to yank sixth chair out from under a mosquito like Eddie.

When she opened the door to the cafeteria, Julep expected to find a hive of stagehands hard at work. She expected to see the actors onstage. She expected Mrs. Picklehaupt to come at her, rattling off a list of things that needed doing. Instead, Julep saw one lone, half-painted, wobbly castle wall. Mrs. Picklehaupt wasn't around. Nor were Danica, Betsy, Ethan, Bernadette, Calvin, or the rest of the cast and crew. Even Trig was missing from his usual lounging table. Where was everybody?

A gingerbread-brown ponytail flew past. "Millie?" called Julep. "Where did everyone go?"

Millie Aldridge swung around. Her eyes were bloodshot and puffy. "Home," she clipped, wiping a red nose on the sleeve of her daisy sweater.

"Mrs. Picklehaupt let everybody leave early?"

"Didn't you hear?" Millie punched the door handle with her palm. "The play's been canceled."

10 To Let It Be Or Not to Let It Be?

"I t's S.N.F.," Julep said, throwing her library book onto the top shelf of her locker so hard it hit the back wall with a hollow *thud*. "I'm the assistant director and nobody said a word to me about canceling the play. How could Mr. Becker do it after all the hard work I've—I mean, we've—done?"

Trig moved his super-duper raspberry-swirl jawbreaker into his right cheek so he could say, "'Cause the principal outranks you."

Peering around her locker door, Julep shot him a nasty look. Boys. Bernadette said they were emotionally stunted from watching football and other violent sports on television. She said sports destroyed the four sensitivity cells they were born with.

Julep stuffed her English homework into her folder. "This whole thing is so not fair—"

"We know," groaned Bernadette. "And we agree with you, but what can we do? Mrs. Picklehaupt is going to have a baby and the doctor says she has to stay in bed until it's born. Mr. Becker told us they're bringing in a substitute teacher to handle Mrs. Pickle-haupt's English classes for the rest of this semester and probably next semester, too, 'cause by then she'll be on maternity leave."

"So why didn't he find someone to take over drama for her?"

"He tried. Nobody could do it on such short notice."

"Or wanted to," interjected Trig.

"You don't seem that upset about it," Julep said to Bernadette. "I mean, your acting dream has shriveled up faster than Cooper's earthworm collection did last summer."

"Thanks for that picture."

"Sorry."

"And who says I'm not upset?" Bernadette frowned. "But griping about it isn't going to change anything. You have to accept—"

"I have to gripe," growled Julep. "I'm really bent that Mrs. Picklehaupt didn't even call me. I'm the—"

"Assistant director," moaned Trig and Bernadette.

"Well, it's soooo not—"

"Don't say it," Bernadette clipped. "Please do not say it again. Nobody's happy about what happened—"

"I'm happy," said Trig.

"You are?"

"Sure. I don't have to paint scenery anymore and I still get my E.C. points. We all do," he said, slapping Julep on the back. "You, too."

She hadn't even given a thought to her extra credit.

Trig chuckled. "How often do you get full credit for doing half the work?"

"In your case, too often," shot Bernadette.

Julep was relieved to know she would get her B-minus in English, but it wasn't enough. She wanted more. She wanted to be assistant director. Julep pulled her terra-cotta bangs straight up into the air. "There has to be something we can do—"

"There isn't," said Bernadette. "Without an adviser we're dead in the water. It's over."

"But what if we—?"

"Let it be. For once, Julep, can't you let something be?" Bernadette shoved her glasses up the bridge of her nose so hard they made a cracking noise.

"Sure." Julep shut her locker and flipped the combination, watching the numbers blur in front of her. "Sure I can," she said quietly.

Bernadette grabbed her oboe and the three of them headed to their first-period classes; Trig and Julep to Mr. Wyatt's for math and Bernadette to honors social studies. The mood spoiled, they mumbled their good-byes.

Julep tried to listen to Mr. Wyatt's lesson on how to multiply decimals, but her mind drifted away. She kept seeing Bernadette's contorted face, kept hearing the *pop* of her glasses, kept remembering those hurtful words. What did she mean "for once, can't you let something be"? When in her life had Julep ever pursued anything? Ask anyone. Even her mother complained that she didn't have "stick-to-itiveness." Why, Julep had failed, quit, or gotten kicked out of everything she'd ever attempted, except for drama club. And the trumpet. Now the play was toes up, and she had a sinking feeling band might not be far behind.

Julep did not say any more to her friends about the play, but she couldn't stop thinking about it. She kept imagining how beautiful the castle set would look once it was finished. She saw the cafeteria brimming with parents, teachers, students, and her family. Everyone was clapping and chanting. "Ju-lep! Ju-lep! Ju-lep!" She could see it. She could actually see it happening.

She was Julep Antoinette O'Toole, Assistant Director. When you've waited eleven years for a title like that, how in the world can you possibly "let it be"?

"Julep, I'm stretched to the limit as it is—"

"It's only for a few weeks. We only want a chance to perform the play," begged Julep, following Mrs. Lindamood around the classroom. Her science teacher placed a booklet about weather forecasting on each empty desk. "Just once."

"Julep, I can't."

"But why not?"

Her teacher stopped short and Julep ran into the back of her denim-blue leather scrunch boots. Turning around, Mrs. Lindamood let out a long, slow breath. Julep knew that sigh. It was the one your teacher gave you when she was trying to be patient but all the caffeine from her morning coffee had worn off and you were squeezing her last nerve. "Here is my after-school schedule: rocket club on Mondays, science club on Thursdays, and open lab every Tuesday and Friday so kids can come in for tutoring or makeup work. See what I mean?"

Mrs. Lindamood really *was* stretched to the limit.

"I am sorry," she said. "I know how disappointing it must be for you to not be able to finish the production. But there's always next year."

Another lame-o cliché! Why did adults always say stuff like that? Next year was twelve long month away, and so much could happen between now and then. Julep was A.D. today. Who knew where or what she would be 365 days from now?

Julep shuffled to the door. "Thanks anyway."

"You'd better hurry. You've already missed most of first lunch."

Julep didn't care. In the hallway, she slipped a piece of pink, strawberry-scented paper from her notebook. Julep had talked to every administrator, teacher, coach, counselor, and librarian at Heatherwood Middle School about taking over drama club. Mrs. Lindamood was the last name on her list. Julep took a felt-tip pen from the zipper pocket of her backpack. "That's it," she said out loud, watching Mrs. Lindamood's name disappear beneath a scrawl of black ink. Now it really was the end. Julep could hear her sister as clearly as if Harmony were standing beside her. "Did you know I beat out three eighth graders to win the starring role in *Pollyanna*?"

Julep clamped her eyes shut.

"And what you have done with your life?"

Nothing. Not one single meaningful thing.

The smell of strawberries must have stirred up something in Julep's brain, because her stomach was starting to gurgle. She was supposed to buy lunch today. No pickled beets on whole wheat or dried seaweed and mustard on pumpernickel. Sweet! Unfortunately, by the time Julep got to the cafeteria all the sausage French-bread pizza was gone. She stared through the glass case at her choices: limp fish sticks or watery chili.

Beans before P.E.? Hello, gaseous anomaly.

"Fish sticks," Julep said to Mrs. Gaffney. She wondered what the Heatherwood cook looked like without that black hairnet squishing down her frosted ash-brown hair. Julep bet that if she ever saw Mrs. Gaffney outside of school, say, buying cat food at Target, she probably wouldn't recognize her without that hairnet.

"Where have you been?" quizzed Bernadette as Julep's tray hit the table.

"Nowhere."

Bernadette tipped her head as if trying to decide whether to press the issue, but decided against it. Julep was glad. She didn't want to think about or talk about drama club anymore. It was done. Finished. A charred blob of ashes. After smothering her fish sticks in bland tartar sauce, Julep cut them into pieces with her plastic spork. She took a bite. It tasted like wet rubber coated with kitty litter, dipped, of course, in bland tartar sauce. And yet, it was tastier than the majority of her mother's dishes.

"Julep, I can't walk home with Cooper and you today," said Trig.

"How come?"

"I'm joining chess club."

"Shouldn't you learn how to play checkers first?" Bernadette giggled.

Clutching his chest, Trig let out a fake laugh. Then he zinged her in the shoulder with a cherry jelly bean.

Bernadette checked her waterproof digital wristwatch that could tell you the time in three different zones. "I have to get going. I've got to check out a camera before lunch ends so I can take pictures in band today. Meet you guys in P.E."

"I'll come with you," said Trig. "I was thinking of joining yearbook, too."

Bernadette snorted. "I'm not doing your layouts for you."

"Did I ask you to?"

"You will."

"Get over yourself, Reed." A red jelly bean bounced off Bernadette's neck. What was it with guys and throwing things?

"Julep, you'll be okay?" asked Bernadette, gathering up stuff. "There's three minutes left until the bell."

Julep gave the pair a lackluster wave with her spork.

It was so easy for them. Bernadette had mourned the death of the play for all of two minutes before hopping on board the yearbook staff. Now Trig was into chess club and, from the sound of things, yearbook, too. Her friends had moved on. Why couldn't she?

Spearing another piece of fish, Julep let her eyes wander over to the next row of tables. Betsy was standing behind Danica, braiding gold beads into her hair. Jillian and Kathleen were squabbling about something—she couldn't hear what, but Jillian's hands were fluttering and Kathleen kept shaking her head. Little purple violets on a vast green pasture passed behind Betsy, who'd stooped to whisper something into Danica's ear. An invisible tarantula climbed Julep's spine.

A bite of soggy fish halfway to her mouth, the idea came to Julep. At first, she dismissed it. It was completely ridiculous. Crazy, is what it was. She blamed it on the rancid fish sticks and tried to forget it. Yet, in the back of her mind Julep knew the truth. A field of violets was her only hope of saving everything that mattered.

11

Catch a Falling Star

6:49 P.M.   Mood: Worried

Dear Amelia:

I put an announcement in the school bulletin that the play is back on again. Robbie Cornfeld read it on the closed-circuit TV this morning in first period. I got so nervous waiting for him to get to it (it was the last one before the lunch menu) I almost P.M.P!

All day, everybody, even Danica, kept bugging me to tell them what was going on, but I didn't crack. I just repeated the announcement that "all cast and crew are to report to the cafeteria after school on Wednesday." I pretended not to know anything. I don't think I fooled my C.B.F. I'm <u>aching</u> to tell them, but I can't risk a leak. I have to Z.M.C.L. or it could ruin everything.

In less than forty-eight hours, I will either be: A) a hero or B) toxic mold. I'm rooting for A, but something tells me B might soon be my middle name. Julep Fungushead O'Toole.

This whole plan could go KA-BOOM at any moment, but I have to try. I think Mrs. Picklehaupt would want me to. Although my friends say they don't care, I think they would want me to. I want me to. Wish me luck. Actually, I don't believe in luck (those of us who get lots of the bad kind never do). Wish me open minds.

C.Y.L.

Julep

Julep's Decoder Page

P.M.P.:   Peed My Pants
C.B.F.:   Co-best Friends
Z.M.C.L.: Ziploc My Chatty Lips

WARNING! READING THIS COULD CAUSE HICCUPS, GAS, RASH, HEADACHES, DIARRHEA, INSOMNIA, OR DEATH BY ANGRY SISTER!

At twenty-two minutes after two on Wednesday afternoon, Julep climbed the steps of the stage. Her back was sweaty. Her fingers were cold. The rest of her was terrified. She knew the students could:

A. Laugh
B. Throw licorice
C. Leave
D. All of the above.

Julep surveyed the group of kids assembled in front of her. The Head Goose, her goslings, Ethan, Calvin, Eddie, Millie, Robbie, Cherry Anne, Tessa—everyone who had worked on the play was curiously gazing back at her. They were waiting for an explanation of why they were here when, only a few days ago, they had been told to go home and forget about the play. Bernadette and Trig were there, too. They were both mad that she had refused to tell them what was going on. Julep regretted that, but there was no other way. Soon, they would see why she had been so secretive. She hoped they'd understand, hoped they wouldn't opt for C or D on the list of possible outcomes. It was, she knew, an enormous risk.

"Hi," said Julep. She fumbled with the zipper on her fleece vest with the monarch butterflies. She pulled it up and down a bunch of times. It got stuck. The back door of the cafeteria opened, letting in a shaft of sunlight. The door closed with a heavy *ka-chung* at the very moment the zipper got free and flew up to Julep's neck.

"Thanks, everybody, for . . . uh . . . for coming," said Julep nervously. "I'm here to tell you that Mr. Becker gave us permission to do the play. I was thinking we could get reorganized today and start rehearsals tomorrow. Mrs. Picklehaupt sent us the box of scripts, so we're ready to go—"

"Whoa, there! Hold your horsies, O'Fool."

Julep rolled her eyes. She ought to have known he wasn't going to make this easy for her.

"Yes, Calvin?"

Calvin Kapinski was perched on the middle table in the second row, though you weren't supposed to sit on top of the tables. "You forgot something."

"What—?" She bit the words *Cootie Face* in half on her tongue.

"The principal said we can't do the play without an adviser."

"I know—"

"So where is he?" Calvin stroked the top of his uneven buzz cut. "Where's the head honcho? The top gun? The big kahuna?"

"Right here," boomed a voice. Everyone turned around. For a moment it seemed as if the sun had dropped out of the sky and landed in the Heatherwood cafeteria. But it wasn't a falling star at all. Bobbing toward them was a yellow orb covered in some 61,760 orange poppies. "I'm your new adviser," said the Lunch Monster, her good eye roving to and fro. "And Mr. Kapinski, you have exactly two seconds to get your rear end off that lunch table."

The Lunch Monster stuck a whistle between her thick lips. She puffed out her cheeks and was about to blow when Julep cried, "Wait!" She tore down the steps. This wasn't how Julep had planned for things to go at all. She was supposed to introduce the Lunch Monster quietly, gradually, so that everyone could warm to the idea of having the scariest adult in school supervising them.

The whistle fell. A pair of shaggy eyebrows turned downward. "Don't you want me to get everyone—?"

"No," said Julep, shrinking at the sight of a giant blister on the Lunch Monster's upper lip. "We know what to do. Everything will be fine."

"Okay, then." Mrs. Flaskin picked up a black leather purse that looked more like carry-on luggage. "I'll be on the couch if you need me."

I won't.

"Thanks," said Julep crisply.

A befuddled cast and crew watched the Lunch Monster toddle to the lumpy cranberry sofa in the back of the room where the cafeteria workers hung out during their breaks. She parked herself in the middle of the cushions and took an iPod out of her handbag. Sticking the earbud headphones in, she began thumbing through an old issue of the *National Enquirer* that someone had left on the couch.

"You have got to be kidding," hissed Calvin as bodies closed in around Julep. "O'Fool, have you completely lost what little mind you have?"

"She won't have to get up off the couch if we behave," whispered Julep. "Besides, we don't have a choice. It's her or nobody."

"I vote nobody," said Betsy. "That eye creeps me out."

"Which one is glass?" asked Ethan.

"The left."

"No, the right," said someone else, and a small squabble broke out.

"The Monster took my trail mix today at lunch," said Jillian, protectively cradling a bag of Doritos. "She'll probably go through our packs and steal stuff while we're rehearsing."

"She will not," said Julep, though, admittedly, the same thought had crossed her mind. She glanced expectantly at the faces around her. "So is everybody in?"

Every head swiveled toward the Lunch Monster. An orthopedic shoe was tapping in time to the iPod. What kind of music, Julep wondered, was the Lunch Monster into? Probably something with an accordion, she figured.

"This is never going to work," said Betsy. "Wait until everyone hears the Lunch Monster is our adviser. We'll be the school joke. Nobody will come to see the play."

A murmur of agreement swept through the crowd. A few kids, like Eddie and Calvin, were already putting on their coats and gathering their gear. A surge of panic went through Julep. Everyone was on the verge of quitting! It was so still in the cafeteria Julep could hear the *tick-tick-tick* of the second hand as it traveled around the clock. She wished someone would say or do something. A single bead of sweat trickled down the back of her neck. Julep felt it slide between her shoulder blades before falling faster down the slope of her back. Her head suddenly felt heavy. Julep let it drop. Maybe it was better this way. She wouldn't have to watch them file out and leave her standing here alone.

A purple blur swished past. Julep looked up. Bernadette was taking a script out of the box. She grinned at Julep. "I'm in," she said.

Yes!

Julep's eyes filled with water. Truthfully, she wasn't sure how her friends would react to the news. But here was her diamond, glistening brighter and lovelier than ever. Hands in his pockets, Trig sauntered over to stand beside Bernadette. Under the pretense of getting an eyelash out of her eye, Julep brushed away her tears. If nobody else came up, if the play died right here and now, it would be all right.

Flipping a lock of strawberry-blond hair behind her ear, Cherry Anne stepped up to the box. Slowly, one by one, the rest of the cast came forward. When Calvin approached, Julep heard him murmur, "We're going down in flames." But he took a script. Jillian and Betsy fought over whose script was whose until Danica yelled from the back of the line, "Oh, will the two of you just take one, already?" Tessa called for everyone on the stage crew to follow her backstage. Trig, Millie, Robbie, Kathleen, and most of the other stagehands went with her. Not everybody stayed. Two seventh-grade stagehands and Joey Morton, an eighth grader with a minor part, walked out. But it could have been a whole lot worse.

Danica was the last person to reach into the box. Her hand came up with a script, and something else: a turquoise fiberglass clipboard. "Here, Julep," she said, holding it out. "You'll need this to direct us."

Julep gulped. "Direct?"

Her tongue turned to shredded wheat. Julep's toes went tingly. And she was certain she'd felt her first-ever pimple explode onto the surface of her chin. Julep had only meant to save the play, not lead it. She had figured that someone else, like Tessa or Cherry Anne, would be in charge. The only thing Julep knew about directing was what she'd picked up watching Mrs. Picklehaupt. And that wasn't much. Kids were looking at her. What was she supposed to do?

Take the clipboard, for starters. Figure out the rest later.

Green eyes met amber ones. As Danica handed her the clipboard, gold charms clinked against the fiberglass rectangle. A dimple appeared in the center of Danica's chin. Julep couldn't remember if she smiled back. Or even if she said anything. She only knew that, for once, Danica did not look away.

12 Preparing for Greatness

That afternoon, Julep didn't find the note until everyone, except Trig and the Lunch Monster, had gone home. At the time, the Lunch Monster was turning off the lights in the cafeteria. Her co-best friend had trotted out to the vending machines in the hallway to get a can of soda pop and wait for her. Julep was heading backstage to put the empty script box in the prop room when a flash of light blue caught her eye. It was an envelope, stuck between the flaps in the bottom of the box. And it had her name on it! Julep set the box on the floor, took out the envelope, and ran her finger along the back flap. She slid out a piece of grayish-blue paper.

Dear Julep:

I am sorry that I had to leave drama club so suddenly, and that I didn't get a chance to explain things or say good-bye. I was delighted, however, to learn that you were determined to carry on (I knew you were a self-starter!). Here are the scripts you'll need to get The Princess and the Pea started again. Please tell Mrs. Flaskin, *the cast, and crew that I am thinking of them, and sending my best wishes for a successful production. I am always here if you need some advice along the way. Don't hesitate to call. Use my favorite clipboard with my blessing!*

Sincerely,
Rita M. Picklehaupt

Julep tried to put the note back in its matching envelope, but her hands were shaking.

She thinks I can do it. She really thinks I can direct. But what if she's wrong? What if I can't?

It was so much pressure. Julep didn't want to disappoint anyone—not Bernadette or Trig or Cherry Anne or her drama teacher. And especially not her family. Not again. Julep was scared to direct. And yet, *not* directing scared her, too.

Giving up on ever getting the note back into the envelope, Julep tucked it into her backpack. She told no one, not even her co-best friends, about it. But when she got home, Julep carefully glued the letter from Mrs. Picklehaupt onto a blank page of her journal. When someone believes in you, and they do it in writing, you keep the proof. You keep it forever.

"Gross, Jules, what's that goop on your face?"

"My secret formula. And you do not have permission to enter my room." Julep caught the slice of cucumber sliding down the side of her face and stuck it back on her eye. With two fingers, she pushed up a glop of white cream that was starting to fall off her cheek.

"Peeee-yeeeeew," yowled Cooper. "You can smell that stuff down the block—"

"Begone, Germ Boy." She flicked her index finger against her thumb.

With the cucumbers covering her eyelids, Julep couldn't tell if her brother had obeyed her or not. But it had gotten quiet. Tomorrow was her first full day as Julep O'Toole, Director. She needed to look her best, which was why she had transformed her bedroom into a minispa. On her dresser, the aromatherapy machine her aunt Ivy had given her for Christmas was churning out a cozy scent of sugar cookies. From the speakers, the soothing voice of Celtic singer Enya was singing "Paint the Sky with Stars." The spa atmosphere had worked so well, Julep had almost fallen asleep, that is, until a certain pain-in-the-rumpus little brother had shown up. The sound of creaking wood told her that she was not yet alone. "Cooper! Get out of my drawers or I'm telling Mom."

"I need a battery for my walkie-talkie."

Julep tore the cucumbers off her eyes and flipped sideways in her furry apricot beanbag chair. "You're not going to be able to walkie or talkie if you don't shut that drawer now. There aren't any batteries in there anyway, so you're wasting your time."

"Hey." Harmony appeared in the doorway. "Do you guys smell rotten—oh. You know, you stink from a block away—"

"That's what I said." Cooper, who had not stopped pawing through Julep's drawer, laughed.

"What is it this time?" asked Julep's sister.

Julep patted her chin. "Butter with sour cream and shredded Cheddar cheese on top." She was beginning to regret putting the butter on first. With her face all greased up, the layer of sour cream kept slipping off. "I got it off the Internet. You're supposed to mix egg whites, butter, cheese, and yogurt. Except we were out of eggs and yogurt. I had to use sour cream instead."

"It's not going to work."

"How would you know?"

"Cooper?" Harmony sat down on the bed, delicately crossing her slim, tanned legs. "Could you please leave me and the human baked potato alone?"

Wiping his snotty nose on his sleeve (thanks to his allergies, Cooper's nose was *always* running), their brother bounced toward the door. Right away, Julep's big-sister radar told her that something was wrong. He was being waaaaay too cooperative.

"Hold it!" she shouted. "Hands up, buddy."

"Aw, geez," he moaned, but didn't resist. Cooper unfolded his fist to reveal he'd swiped her light-up plastic butterfly that flashed when you shook it. Caught in the act, he plopped it on her desk.

Once Cooper was gone, Harmony turned her attention to Julep. "How many times do I have to tell you that no matter what you do, you can't get rid of freckles?"

"Can so." Julep settled deeper in her beanbag chair and put the cucumber slices back on her eyes. "I just haven't found the right recipe yet, that's all."

"What's the big deal? So you've got a few—"

"Eighty-seven. I have eighty-seven freckles."

"Good to see you're not obsessing over it. Julep, lots of people have them. It's no big thing."

Julep knew it would be a colossal thing to Harmony if she had nearly a hundred little brown spots all over her cheeks and nose, and a gooberhead like Calvin was forever teasing her about them. "Did you know that if you connect the dots on Julep's face you get a picture of a monkey?" Calvin had said once right in the middle of silent reading. Then he scratched under his arms and made monkey hooting sounds. True, Mr. Donnelly had given him detention. Calvin had to stay after school for one afternoon, but Julep had suffered for far longer. For months afterward, kids called her Freckle Face Monkey. Oh, yeah, freckles were no big thing.

Harmony sighed. "You've tried practically everything in the fridge. What's left?"

She had a point. Julep had spent the last two years experimenting with a variety of ingredients to come up with a formula that would remove or, at least, fade her hated freckles: lemon juice, lime juice, lemon *and* lime juice together (two items that should never be used if you have a slight cut on your face—zouch!), honey, ketchup, egg whites, radish juice, parsley leaves, and toothpaste. None of them worked. However, the toothpaste did leave her face smelling minty fresh for three whole days afterward.

"Julep, it's time to put on your big-girl pants and deal with it." Harmony proudly rattled off her newest saying. "You have freckles. It's a fact."

Julep didn't want to deal with it. What she wanted was silky-smooth, pale, freckle-free skin. Tomorrow was going to be the biggest day of her life. Nothing could be left to chance. She was about to explain this to Harmony when she felt an odd pinging sensation on her face and neck. Pushing the cucumbers from her eyes, Julep saw a shower of brown flecks coming directly at her. The tidbits stung her forehead, nose, cheeks, and chin. "Ow, ow, ow," she yelped with each ping. A moment before she got hit directly in the eye, Julep saw a devious face above her. "You can't be a real baked potato," cried Cooper, shaking the jar again, "without bacon bits!"

9:09 P.M.   Mood: Eager

Dear Amelia:

I'm ready for my first full day as Play Director! I have all the necessary equipment:

I have smooth skin, un-puffy eyes, and unfortunately, a zillion fake bacon bits in my hair (you didn't really think my mom would buy REAL bacon bits, did you?). I'm still trying to get them all out. Don't worry, Cooper will pay.

Sadly, my secret freckle formula didn't work. I'm not giving up. On behalf of freckle-faced girls like me everywhere, I will keep trying until not one pesky brown dot remains!

'Night,

Julep

HAT

CLIPBOARD

PEANUT
BUTTER
CRACKERS &
CHOCOLATE
MILK

DIRECTOR'S CHAIR

P.S. What <u>are</u> fake bacon bits made from?
Does anybody anywhere really know?

13   A Born Leader

"How about now? How does it look now, Julep?" Millie's voice bounced off the cafeteria ceiling.

"It's blocking the castle entrance. Go stage left a few more feet."

Millie, her back to Julep, lifted the papier-mâché bush and began moving the wrong way. Julep started to point that out but was interrupted.

"Are we going to start anytime this century?" Betsy was leaning against the wall, lower body jutted out and arms folded in front.

Julep checked her mother-of-pearl bracelet watch. They'd already wasted fourteen minutes of valuable rehearsal time. "All actors, get over here," she called.

Grinning broadly, Bernadette dropped her backpack and flew to Julep. Betsy scooted down the wall a foot. But that was about it for a response. Jillian didn't budge from in front of a round hand mirror she'd propped up on a table. Cherry Anne kept puttering around backstage. Calvin, Eddie, Ethan, and a few other boys continued flying paper airplanes at the rear of the cafeteria. How was Julep supposed to direct if nobody would do what she told them to do?

Julep glanced back at the lumpy cranberry couch. The Lunch Monster had spread her mammoth self out over the cushions. Poor cushions. Poor helpless suffocated cushions. They had sunk so deeply into the springs they were no longer visible. The Lunch Monster was listening to her iPod and flipping through a copy of *People*.

Julep waved her clipboard in the air. "Come on, everyone. Please?"

"We can't start yet," said Jillian. "Danica's in the hall practicing."

"So go get her," replied Betsy.

Jillian was putting a zigzag part in her hair. "You get her."

"No, you."

"No, you."

"*Somebody,* get her," said Julep. It felt like a hippopotamus had sat down right between her eyes.

"Fine," said Betsy. "I'll do it. Unlike some people"—she stuck her tongue out at Jillian then turned to Julep—"I'm here to help."

"Tessa!" Julep called out to the set designer scurrying past. "Where is the bed frame?"

"My dad's still building it."

"When will it be here?"

Tessa spun, continued trotting backward, and lifted a shoulder. "When it's finished."

"But we need it—"

"How about now?" Millie turned around to ask again.

Julep squinted. "Stage *left.*"

"I went left."

"You're facing the back of the stage. So stage left is your right."

Millie groaned. "Then why didn't you say my right?"

"It's not director lingo," drawled Trig, from somewhere to Julep's right. Or was it her left?

Bernadette's nose twitched. "Did they serve B.L.T.s for lunch today? It smells like bacon in—"

"No," snapped Julep. She ran a hand through her hair. Nothing resembling bacon bits fell out. Big relief.

"Can I help?" asked Bernadette, at her elbow.

"No thanks."

"How about if I make a list of the cast and crew? We could turn it in to Mrs. Holcomb so she could get started designing the play programs."

The programs! Julep had forgotten about them. "Did it," she lied.

"How about if I write up something about the play for Robbie to read in the morning announcements?" pressed Bernadette. "You know, to get people to come to see us?"

"Taken care of." Another lie.

Shielding her clipboard from the More Girl's prying eyes, Julep added the words *programs* and *bulletin announcement* to the bottom of the page. Starting from the top, she began numbering the items on a to-do list that was growing by the second.

"This is such a blastoid." Bernadette giggled. "You get to be the director, I get to be an actress, and we get to put on the play all by ourselves for the whole school. Isn't this a blastoid?"

"Yeah."

. . . six, seven, eight . . .

"You know what would really be a blastoid? If we could put on the play for the kids at Valley View."

. . . eleven, twelve . . .

"We could go over there during the day—wait, I know." She snapped her fingers. "We could bring them over here, which would be easier 'cause the set's here. I bet the little kids would love to see *The Princess and the Pea.* Don't you think? Wouldn't Cooper think it was a blastoid to see his big sister direct a play?"

. . . eighteen, nineteen, twenty . . .

"Julep?"

"Uh-huh?"

Twenty-three things.

Crunch! Another hippopotamus collapsed onto Julep's head.

"Wouldn't he?"

"Wouldn't who?"

Bernadette raised an eyebrow. "You're sure there's nothing I can do?"

You mean besides stop saying the word blastoid?

Julep pasted a grin on her throbbing face. "Positive."

"We're heeeeere!" screeched Betsy, following the Head Goose into the cafeteria. "Can you please get rehearsal started, Julep, before, like, my wisdom teeth grow in?"

Twirling toward Julep, Bernadette crossed one eye and flicked her hair back. "Yes," she said, quietly mimicking Betsy's voice. "Could we please get rehearsal started before, like, my diva head explodes?"

Julep let out a laugh at her friend's dead-on impression of Gosling Number One, but quickly regained her composure. She had twenty-three things to accomplish. There was no time to goof off. She clapped her hands. "Actors onstage, please. We're going straight through the play. Scripts are okay for now."

Tucking the turquoise clipboard under one arm, Julep strolled to her metal folding chair. She'd set it up in an aisle about halfway between the stage and the lunch counter. A small square of neon-yellow posterboard was tacked to the back of the chair with masking tape. It was a last-minute gift from her family this morning. In Harmony's neat block print the bright orange letters read: **JULEP O'TOOLE: DIRECTOR.**

Taking a seat in *her* chair, Julep leaned back. She snapped a mental picture of the scene before her. She didn't want to forget anything that was about to happen from this point forward. Julep might have a raging headache and twenty-three tasks to complete and a few uncooperative kids, but she wasn't going to let such minor things stand in the way of feeling the exhilaration, the satisfaction, the sheer *power* of being a director.

Move over, Steven Spielberg. Step aside, George Lucas.

Julep raised her clipboard.

The mighty Julep O'Toole has arrived!

"Cherry Anne?" Julep stopped the narrator in the middle of her introduction. "Let's move you to the top step of the stage, okay?"

"But Mrs. Picklehaupt told me to stand here."

"I know, but nobody can see you on the second step. Go up two steps."

"But Mrs. Picklehaupt—"

"Pleeeease?"

Cherry Anne said she would, and Julep felt a tingle zip up her arms. It was joy. Pure joy. Pure director's joy. And, for a brief moment, it numbed the pounding in her head. With a waggle of her clipboard, she started them again.

"How about now?" came a hiss in her ear. "Sorry," said Millie, catching a startled Julep before she tipped over in her chair. "How does everything look?"

Righting herself, Julep inspected the papier-mâché trees, bushes, and flowers surrounding the castle. "Looks good," she whispered back. "But why is that top castle window on the left only half-painted?"

"Stage left?"

"No, left left." She massaged her temple. "Stage right, I mean."

"Trig was supposed to do it."

"Where is he?" Julep asked, though she already knew. For several minutes, she had heard a noise that sounded like a bicycle tire with a slow leak coming from a few rows over.

When Millie skipped away, Julep got up. She tiptoed past the Lunch Monster's black dress with, oh, a good 55,950 hearts on it (without going over). Closing in on the whistling sound, Julep saw the soles of Trig's Nikes sticking out beyond the end of the row. She found her co-best friend lying on his back across three of the connecting benches attached to the lunch tables. His hands were folded neatly on top of his chest. Under cover of his Mariners baseball cap, he was softly snoring. Ordinarily, she would have laughed. Today, with so much work to do, it wasn't funny.

Tie his shoelaces together. Put a wet finger in his ear. Scream at the top of your lungs. Just get him up.

Julep stood there.

Wake up, Trig. Wake up, will you? Please?

After a few minutes, Julep padded away. She could feel the Lunch Monster's good eye following her back to her chair. Julep didn't care. What did somebody like the Lunch Monster know about directing? What did she know about friendship?

"Follow me, please," Betsy said, sticking her arm straight out to the side.

"Cut," cried Julep, flagging her down with her clipboard.

"What?" Betsy glared. The arm remained at attention.

"You probably shouldn't do that."

"Do what?" The glare deepened. The stiff arm did not fall.

"You're overdoing with the arm. Be yourself. Be natural."

"But Mrs. Picklehaupt—"

"Isn't here," shouted Julep, a thunderbolt of pain piercing her skull. If one more person started a sentence with the words *But Mrs. Picklehaupt* she was going to rip out every last follicle of hair on her head. And she had a LOT of follicles to work with. "I'm the director, remember?" She waved her clipboard.

"Yeah, she's the director," said Calvin, holding up his arm and waggling his script like a clipboard. How rude! Pretty soon, everyone on the stage had their arms in the air, waving their scripts, too. Well, almost everyone. Bernadette didn't join in; however, she did pull her hair across her face—her signature move to hide a grin.

Real mature, people. Real mature. Ignore them. They'll quit when they see it isn't bothering you. Pretend you don't see it.

Julep hopped to her feet and took a brisk stroll around her folding chair.

La-dee-dee. I don't see anything. I do not see Calvin shaking his rear or Eddie pretending to be a helicopter. I don't even see Jillian talking on her cell phone.

Julep had circled her chair four times when Cherry Anne said, "All right, guys, let's stop playing around."

"Why?" asked Calvin. "It is a play, after all. If you can't play while doing a play then where else can you play?"

"Say that ten times fast," dared Betsy.

That's all it took for the cast and crew to completely let loose. Everyone began talking at once, trying to outdo one another by saying Calvin's tongue twister as quickly as possible. From where Julep stood, it sounded like Ethan—no, make that the hyper Millie—was the winner. Julep sank into her seat. The clipboard clattered to the floor.

Does Steven Spielberg have it this rough?

Her first day as a director wasn't turning out anything like she'd planned. Where was the exhilaration? The power? The respect? Where, more importantly, was the aspirin? Maybe she was trying too hard, expecting too much. It was, after all, their very first day back. Everyone was enthusiastic, nervous, and talkative. Or disorderly, uncontrollable, and loudmouthed if you were sitting in a metal chair with your name on the back in bright orange letters.

Don't freak out. Give them time. In a day or two, they will settle in. And settle down. Then we'll really get things done around here. We'll show everyone we can do this play on our own. Mrs. Picklehaupt will be so proud of me—of us.

The throbbing from within Julep's skull was so intense it threatened to hammer her eyeballs out. She closed her eyes and rested her forehead in her hands. Tomorrow, things will be different, she told herself. Tomorrow, everything will be one day better.

A paper airplane bounced off her ear.

Shortly after that, the sign fell off the back of her chair.

14 IS It JUSt Me?

$\mathcal{J}$ulep floated forward and back, letting the tips of her toes drag in the muddy rut. It was Friday afternoon, and instead of going home after play rehearsal, she had come here. Something had drawn her across the parking lot to Valley View Elementary. Julep had gone to her old school and her favorite swing—second one from the end across from the tall oak tree. The black U-shaped rubber seat wasn't too high or too low. The chains rarely kinked up. It flew straighter and higher than any of the others. Comfortable and familiar, this swing was everything that middle school wasn't.

The rain against her skin, the cold metal chains, the mud under her toes—it all felt good. Julep had loved most everything about elementary school, especially Mrs. Alden, her fifth-grade teacher. Mrs. Alden always made sure Julep had enough lunch money and her coat buttoned properly and had turned in her library books on time. Middle school wasn't like that. Nobody cared if you ate lunch or got stuck in a tent raincoat or had library books that were three weeks overdue. You were on your own. With six different classes and six different teachers, Julep felt like she was always running to keep up. It left her dizzy and exhausted and longing to be a fifth grader again in a warm, safe classroom. Did anybody else feel this way?

Julep knew that, unlike elementary school, no one at Heatherwood was going to tell her she was a fabulous director. Because middle school was all about harsh realities. And the truth was she wasn't even close to fabulous. The play was falling apart around her and she didn't have a clue as to how to fix it.

After a week and a half of rehearsals, things had not improved. In fact, they had gotten worse. Kids were showing up late, goofing off, and skipping out early. Some, like Cherry Anne, rarely came at all. She'd gotten the soup (or soap) commercial. Despite her threats to take their scripts away for good, the actors didn't seem concerned about learning their lines. Dress rehearsal was set for next Wednesday, with the performance the following Saturday night. They weren't even close to being ready.

Bernadette's constant crowing was also wearing Julep down. "Can I help? Can I help? Can I help?" It was relentless. Why couldn't the More Girl leave her alone for sixty seconds? She was beginning to think Bernadette was trying to snatch her job away so she could take credit for something else she was better at doing than Julep. Trig continued to nap through rehearsals. The only person who *was* cooperating was Betsy Foster. Who'd have thought it? Gosling Number One arrived on time, stayed focused, and was even polite to Julep. It was weird—weird in that parallel-universe kind of way.

Julep spun the swing to her right, using her feet to twirl in circles. When the tightening chains wouldn't let her do one more circle, she lifted her feet. The chains unwound, whipping her wildly round and round. Everything became a blur.

"Weeeeee!" Julep tipped backward and let the blood flow to her brain. It felt great to pretend she had nothing to worry about beyond this moment, nothing but having fun. Naturally, it didn't last.

The worst part was that even the Lunch Monster could tell the play was in trouble. Today, she had come to Julep at the beginning of rehearsal and asked, "Do you need a hand getting everyone quieted down and ready to work?"

"No, no," Julep said, not looking up from her clipboard. She could not be seen conversing with the Lunch Monster, for fear of losing the few drops of respect it had taken her eight days to earn from the cast and crew. Julep held her breath and used all of her brain power to send the Lunch Monster a mental message.

Go to the couch.

The Monster surveyed the kids draped over the tables and the partially constructed castle. She scratched one of her four chins. "Seems a little disorganized."

"Everything's fine."

Go to the couch. Go to the couch. Go to the couch.

After hesitating a moment, the Lunch Monster dug a giant Hershey bar out of her big purse and made her way to the couch. Unfortunately, Julep had less luck getting Calvin and Eddie and the rest of their air band to do what she asked. They refused to put their invisible guitars away. Boiling, Julep had almost walked out. Not that it would have mattered if she had. Nobody would have noticed.

Julep put her shoes into the rut to stop the swing.

"I hate this!" she shouted at the birch trees on the other side of the chain-link fence. "I can't do this! I CANNOT DO THIS."

The trees swayed in the wind, hundreds of leaves applauding. "We know," they said. "We know."

Julep slid off the rubber seat. She'd better get home. Julep went to get her bulging backpack from the base of the swing set. Slinging it over her left shoulder, she grimaced. With her English, math, and science textbooks stuffed inside the nylon pack along with their matching notebooks, crammed with handouts, assignments, reports, and tests, her backpack was usually quite heavy by the end of the week. That was another thing. Nobody ever tells you that once you start middle school you have to carry your life on your back. It hurts. In more ways than one.

Julep's mom glanced up from wiping down the granite countertop. Under the glow of the stove light, she'd been watching Julep's fuzzy green socks glide back and forth in front of the phone. "It's not going to leap into your hand," she said quietly.

Deep in her thoughts, while chewing off her left pinkie nail, Julep didn't realize she was being scrutinized.

"Did you get into an argument with Bernadette?"

"No."

"Trig?"

"Nope," said Julep, munching on the nub of nail that remained. *Not yet.* She was trying to get up the nerve to call him so they could talk about his drama-club sleeping habits. That topic, she knew, could very easily turn into a fight.

"Are you feeling all right?"

"Yeah."

"You look flushed." Her mom came over to feel her forehead. "You *are* a bit warm."

Really? Maybe she was coming down with some disease, some type of rare tropical fever that would require her to remain under quarantine, say, until the end of eighth grade.

Her mom filled a glass with organic papaya juice. Handing it to her daughter, she asked, "Did you bring home your trumpet?"

"Noooo," she said into the glass, her hands feeling the vibration of her words.

"Julep, this is the second weekend in a row you've left it at school."

"My backpack was too full. I can't carry everything."

"Then you should have taken a lighter instrument."

"Mom, you don't take an instrument based on its weight."

"And you don't leave your trumpet at school when you have challenges next week."

Julep didn't know how to break it to her mother or Mr. Dellabalma, but she had no plans to "challenge up." Forget her teacher's advice to practice an hour a day, Julep had not practiced at *all* since her last lesson. With the play, who had time?

"So how's the play going?" Her mother had an annoying knack for reading her mind.

Julep drained the glass. "It's going." She probably should

have put more pep into it, but it was the end of the week and she was running a quart low on pep.

"Speaking of which, I have something for my daughter, the director." Her mother giggled. "Close your eyes."

Julep did as she was told. Sort of. She kept her right eye slightly open to watch her mom tiptoe to the bench by the kitchen door and pop open her briefcase. Her mom bent over and reached inside. Shoot! Her body was blocking the present. When her mother turned around, both of Julep's eyes were securely shut.

"You can look now."

Two white Persian-cat socks were dangling in front of her.

"Thanks, Mom," she said, putting the knitted material to her cheek. Oh, how she had missed her favorite cat socks!

"You can wear them to the premiere of the play. Which reminds me, I have another surprise for you."

"Yeah?"

"Aunt Ivy will be there next Saturday night."

"Aunt I . . . Ivy is coming? From Birch Bay?" Her aunt's alpaca ranch was two hours away. Julep had assumed that her favorite aunt wouldn't be able to make the play. Julep sagged into one of the kitchen chairs. Aunt Ivy, the one person who thought Julep was truly wonderful, was going to see the whole catastrophe unfold in person. She was going to discover the truth about her beloved niece. How depressing.

"You don't think she'd miss your directing debut, do you? We can't wait to see your name in lights—Julep O'Toole, Director." Her mother threw a hand in the air, and drew it across the stove light, making a theater marquee. The pride in her voice only added to Julep's misery. "But I'll settle for seeing it printed in the program."

The program! Julep was supposed to turn in the list of cast and crew to Mrs. Holcomb this afternoon. It had completely slipped her mind.

". . . won't we, Julep?"

"What?"

"I asked if we could get some extra programs."

Julep blew air out of her cheeks. "I hope so."

"I want to send one to your great-aunt Lurlene, and my cousin Wade and his family, oh, and we'll want one for Grandma Miriam and Grandpa Horace, of course . . ."

9:26 P.M.   Mood: Doomed

Dear Amelia:

I am DREADING the next four days. Tomorrow is dress rehearsal. We aren't going to have any programs. I tried to turn in the list today, but Mrs. Holcomb said it was too late. My mom is going to be really disappointed in me. S.W.E.I.N?

I miss drama club. B.I.W.D., I mean. Here are the things I miss:

☺ The way Mrs. Picklehaupt's shoes went smick—smack against the floor

- Mrs. Picklehaupt
- Cracking jokes with Bernadette
- Running lines with Danica
- Papier-mâché (S.S.)

At least when I was working on the
sets the worst thing that could
happen was papier-mâchéing myself
and ruining my cat socks. Now I'm ruining an entire play. I.G.B!

C.Y.L. (if I survive!),

Julep

Julep's Decoder Page

S.W.E.I.N.: So What Else Is New?

B.I.W.D.: Before I Was Director

S.S.: Surprise! Surprise!

I.G.B.: I'm Going Bananas

TWO, FOUR, SIX, EIGHT,
TOUCH MY STUFF AND YOU'RE FISH BAIT!

That evening, before putting her journal away, Julep flipped back a few pages. She ran her finger along the scalloped edge of Mrs. Picklehaupt's grayish-blue stationery and re-read the note. Julep sat up. The last few lines had caught her eye:

I am always here if you need some advice along the way. Don't hesitate to call.

Did her drama teacher mean it? Maybe *don't hesitate to call* was another one of those things that adults said to be polite, not because they truly meant it. But Mrs. Picklehaupt had, after all, written her phone number on the bottom of the page. People didn't give you their phone numbers if they weren't sincere, right?

I could sure use some advice about now.

Julep jumped up.

No, you'll be admitting you can't do it.

Julep sat back down on her bed.

Don't call. Mrs. Picklehaupt has enough to worry about with her baby. She doesn't need you bothering her, too. You're the director. That's what she'll tell you. You're the director. You figure it out. Don't call.

At least, that's what you tell yourself when you don't want to let down the one person in the world who thinks you are smart and a self-starter; the one person who lent you her treasured clipboard; the one person who sees something in you that nobody else, not even you, sees. That's what you tell yourself: don't call. Then you shut your journal. You brush your teeth. You go to bed. And you stare at the ceiling for three and a half hours.

15 When You Look Good, You Feel Good (and Other Lies)

here you are my dear, loving, *generous* sister." Julep oozed all things angelic. "I was wondering, would you—?"

"No." Harmony was inches from the bathroom mirror, applying her third layer of black mascara. She had her mouth in an O shape. This stance always puzzled Julep. Why did you have to open your mouth like a goldfish to paint your eyelashes?

"You didn't let me finish." Julep pouted.

"I'm one step ahead of you, Potato Face."

"But you said I could borrow clothes once in a while—"

"I meant once a year. Twice tops."

"Come on, Harmony, today is the dress rehearsal for the play."

The mascara wand froze. Harmony could hardly deny it was important to look your best on such a big day.

Julep clasped her hands together. "Pleeeeeeeease?"

"What do you want?"

"Your peach floral skirt."

"Ehhh," the sister buzzer sounded. "Try again."

"Burgundy velvet jumper?"

"No, but you can have the black jumper with the metal belt."

And look like a Pilgrim? No thanks. "How about your pink Eiffel Tower dress?"

"Red corduroys with the lace trim on the pockets."

"Khaki safari vest and capri pants."

"Yellow-and-green plaid skort."

They looked at each other in the mirror and shivered. The glow-in-the-dark skort was a gift from Great-Aunt Lurlene. Neither of them would even try it on for fear of being transported to dork land on a one-way bus.

"It has to be something halfway decent, otherwise I'd wear my own stuff," said Julep.

"Blue polka-dot dress."

"Polka dots are for babies. I'm not in the fifth gr—"

Wait a minute. She had it!

"What about your brown suede skirt?" The soft A-line skirt was the color of aged parchment paper. Very stylish. Very sophisticated. Very director-like. "I could wear it with my red frilly shirt and cowboy boots. Wouldn't that be perfect?"

Harmony admitted it would, but still wasn't ready to part with it. "It took me four months of babysitting to buy that skirt. Plus, it's dry-clean only—"

"I won't get anything on it."

"You always say that and you always do."

"I really and truly promise this time."

"I don't know—"

"Don't you see? If I dressed like a real director, maybe everyone would—" She stopped abruptly.

Harmony screwed the wand back into its silver tube. "Okay," she said quietly. "You can wear it."

Bouncing, Julep held up her hand. "I swear I won't stain it. I'll even skip lunch if you want me to stay out of the cafeteria."

After seriously considering that proposal, her sister said, "You'd better eat. I don't want you fainting from hunger, falling on the floor, and getting gum and dirt all over my skirt. Just be careful with it, Julep. Very *very* careful."

"I will guard it with my life."

Why is that whenever you wear something totally beautiful and totally expensive and totally not yours, you feel like a totally different person? You walk taller. You look prettier. You radiate confidence. Everyone notices the transformation.

Julep was a step behind Trig, heading into first-period math when someone spun her around. "I looooooove this," squealed Betsy, flaring out the skirt as if she were thinking about buying it, or ripping it off Julep's body. "Cute cowboy boots, too."

"Um, thanks."

"I'm so excited about dress rehearsal today. I brought my costume."

"I hope everyone else did, too." Julep was concerned about what Calvin was going to show up in, if he showed up at all. Yesterday, in the hall, she had overheard him say something about a Viking helmet. Julep started to go into her classroom when Betsy wrapped an arm around her neck. "I wanted to say that, you know, if something happens today I'm ready."

What did she mean by that? What was going to happen?

"Okay," said Julep warily.

"I know everybody's lines by heart. *Everybody's.*" Betsy put her hand in Julep's and squeezed. "This is for you."

The bell rang. With a parting "Aloha," Betsy flitted across the hall to Mr. Reardon's class. Julep stood there for a moment, half expecting Gosling Number One to come back. She didn't, of course. When Julep looked down, she saw she was holding a bent rope of red licorice.

Toss it. Don't even think about eating it. Toss it.

"Julep?" It was Mr. Wyatt, motioning for her to come into class and take her seat.

"Coming." Julep bit into the twisted rope and immediately wished she hadn't. It was old. And took forever to chew. Hours later, she was still trying to pick sticky bits of it out of her teeth.

"What's up?" asked Trig. "You're looking at your lunch like it's a land mine."

Julep, who was leaning as far back from the table as possible, sat up a bit. She figured the farther away she positioned herself from food, the less likely she was to spill, drizzle, fling, or drop something on her sister's precious suede skirt. She didn't tell that to Trig. To him, she merely said, "Brussels-sprouts-and-goat-cheese pita." He congratulated himself on recognizing that her lunch was, indeed, highly toxic.

"I've invented a new concoction."

The news sent Julep lurching back once again. Next to her, Bernadette did the same.

Trig read their faces. "Chill. I didn't bring it to school."

"Major relief," mumbled Bernadette, pulling the breading

off her corn dog to eat first. She always preferred to eat her way to the center of things.

"It's my greatest concoction yet," he boasted. "But I don't want to spoil the surprise—"

"If it's anything like your tuna on a stick, you're probably too late."

"You'll be eating those words, Reed, when I win the Young Chefs of America regionals with my original recipe."

"As long as I don't have to eat your concoction, I'll be happy."

"As long as I don't have to watch you act, I'll be happy."

Bernadette stopped undressing her corn dog. "What do you mean by that?"

"Nothing." Trig took a bite of his cheeseburger.

"Are you talking about the play?" She pointed her half-naked hot dog at him. "Are you saying that I'm not a good actress? For your information, my director thinks I'm good, don't you, Julep?"

Julep hadn't been paying attention. She was too busy watching the Head Goose watch her. Ever since Julep had sat down, Danica had been stealing glimpses at her. She was, no doubt, admiring Julep's stylish outfit.

Bernadette was nudging her. "Am I or am I not a good actress?"

There it was again! Danica had turned away from Betsy to glance in Julep's direction. What was going on?

"You're okay," Julep answered absently, trying to pretend she hadn't seen Danica spy on her.

Bernadette dropped her corn dog.

Trig shot up an arm in victory. "Ah, I didn't mean it, Reed," he said to a sulking Bernadette. "I was only trying to give as good as I got. How about some ice cream? My treat."

"I don't want any."

"Come on, it's blueberry-cheesecake swirl today—your favorite."

"With rainbow dots?" When he nodded, Bernadette managed a small smile. "Okay."

"Julep, do you want one, too?"

She did, but didn't dare chance it while residing in Harmony's skirt. One blue dribble of blueberry-cheesecake swirl on the parchment-brown suede and her sister would make cheesecake out of her. "No thanks," said Julep. She started to tear open her bag of beet chips with her teeth when she realized her co-best friend was staring at her—actually, the term *glowering* was more accurate—through a pair of smudged glasses. With the corner of the bag still in her teeth, Julep arched her eyebrows. "What?"

"Okay?" bit Bernadette. "Just o-kay?"

Julep let go of the plastic. "I meant that you're, you know, good."

"You didn't say good. You could have said good. But you didn't. You said okay, which is definitely not the same as good."

"Sorry, Bern. I didn't say it right. You *are* a good actress. Great, in fact."

"Thank you." Bernadette gave her a "was that so hard?" sigh.

If her stomach hadn't been trying to digest a few mouthfuls of

Brussels sprouts and stinky cheese, if Danica's sneak peeks hadn't been so distracting, if she wasn't so concerned about preserving Harmony's skirt, Julep would have probably stopped there. She *should* have stopped there. Instead, she added on one teeny tiny word, a three-letter conjunction known for its ability to stir up a whole lot of trouble. Tipping her head, Julep said, "But . . ."

Bernadette wriggled her glasses up her nose. "What?"

"I didn't say anything."

"You said but."

Julep had certainly thought it. Had she said it? Apparently, so. "It's . . . it's a small thing really, so microscopic it's hardly worth mentioning."

Brown eyes became slits. "So mention it."

"Sometimes, I mean, every once in a while . . . not every day or anything, but now and then when you're saying your lines, you kind of, I mean, you sort of—"

"What?"

"Spit."

"Spit?"

"Not all the time," Julep hurried to clarify. "Only when you pronounce your *s*'s and *t*'s and occasionally a *sh*. Then little bits of saliva fly out."

Bernadette slapped a hand over her mouth.

"They're more like sprinkles, really," Julep said. "Tiny saliva sprinkles. Even smaller than sprinkles. Sprinklets, I'd call them."

Two fingers parted. "You know I have this space between my front teeth. I can't help it."

"It's no big deal—"

"Except that everyone thinks I'm a sprinkler."

"Not everyone. I'm sure I'm the only one who's noticed," she lied. "It doesn't bother me that you're a sprinkler, I mean, a spitter—"

"I have to go and . . . um . . . check out a camera," Bernadette mumbled between her fingers.

"Bernadette, I didn't mean—"

"I know what you meant." One hand firmly clamped on her mouth, she grabbed her tray and got up. The end of the tray without support sagged. The fruit cup tipped over. Chunks of peaches, pears, and pineapples tumbled off the tray and onto the table. Julep immediately flew over to the next bench. By the time she was certain none of the fruit or sticky syrup had found its way onto her skirt, her co-best friend was already to the end of their row.

Bernadette barreled toward the trash cans, but was intercepted by the Lunch Monster's light aqua dress sporting about, oh, 26,425 brown bunnies. Licking her scaly lips, Mrs. Flaskin reached out for the partially eaten, naked corn dog on the green tray, but Bernadette was ready. She zigged left, threw out an arm, and flipped her tray. The corn dog, along with the rest of her lunch, slid through Mrs. Flaskin's plump fingers and into the trash can. Bernadette flung her tray on the stack and stalked out the side door.

Julep plopped her elbow onto the table and rested her chin on her palm. What had she been thinking? Bernadette was an overachieving, people-pleasing, perfection-seeking student. She went berserk if she missed even one question on a math quiz. Somebody like the More Girl could not be expected to cope well with saliva issues. Julep, as her best friend, ought to have remembered that. Julep hoped Bernadette would give her the chance to apologize when they saw each other in fifth-period P.E.

"Julep?"

"Hi, Danica," said Julep, a bit startled to see the Head Goose standing next to her. She fanned out her suede skirt in preparation for a compliment. Frankly, she was wondering why it was coming so late. The day was half over.

Danica put a hand on her hip and her charm bracelet slid down over her wrist. "I'm quitting the play."

Julep was aghast. "What? Why?"

"You know what and you know why!" With a wild flip of her black hair, she spun on the heel of one of her designer clogs with the sheepskin lining and marched away. Had Trig not dodged to his left, Danica would have bashed straight into him. They both came within an inch of getting covered in blueberry-cheesecake-swirl ice cream.

"She was sure hauling," said Trig. "Must be a makeup emergency, huh? Another layer of lip gloss, doctor, stat!"

"She quit the play."

"Yeah?" A cone in each hand, he was looking around for Bernadette. "How come?"

Watching the Head Goose and her goslings glide out of the cafeteria in single file, Julep shook her terra-cotta head. "I wish I knew."

16 Wizzle Hair and Seventh Chair

Julep tried to talk to both Bernadette and Danica during P.E. but The Borg had other ideas. After their series of stretches, she informed them they were going to run around the track three times, or three-quarters of a mile! Naturally, it was raining outside—not a heavy downpour so your parents could call the principal and report child abuse, but just enough so that when your kinky hair dried you looked like you'd stuck your finger in the toaster.

On the track, Julep deliberately started at the back of the pack so she could be the passer, not the passee. There was nothing quite as embarrassing as being out in front and watching everyone else breeze by you as you lost steam. Julep hadn't made one complete loop when her chest started to hurt. By the end of the second lap, the wind and drizzle—the wizzle—was blurring her eyesight. In a blaze of brown hair, Bernadette lapped her without even saying hi. Julep dragged herself around the track on the third lap, certain that she'd punctured a lung or some other valuable internal organ. She came in second to last. Only Felice Haynes, whose right leg was shorter than her left, was slower. Trig, as was his custom, never stepped outside to feel the wizzle on his face. He'd produced a note from his doctor that said he was still recovering from triple pneumonia (was there even such a thing?) and was, under no circumstances, supposed to jog.

The first bell had already rung by the time Julep stumbled into the girls' locker room barely clinging to life. Bernadette and Danica had long since left. Julep took a ten-second shower and dressed at record speed, but was still late to sixth period. Fortunately, Miss Crosetti was preoccupied with organizing the percussion section and didn't notice a trumpet case with cowboy boots sneaking into the band room late. Julep slipped into the last chair in the fourth row next to Eddie Levitt. He took one look at her wizzled head and said, "Nice hairdo, Jiffy Pop."

"Eat worms."

Miss Crosetti was still talking to the drummers, so Julep took the opportunity to creep to the front of the room.

Julep crouched beside her friend's music stand. "Bernadette!"

"What is it now?" Bernadette was putting her oboe together and refused to look at her. "Did I spit on you as I ran past? I am *so* sorry if I did."

"I wanted to say—"

"Whoa!" Bernadette got her first glimpse of Julep. "What happened to your hair? It's all poofed—ahhhhh, the rain," she said sadly. Normally, a pity party thrown by the More Girl would have irritated Julep. But if she had to choose between anger and sympathy from her co-best buddy, she'd take sympathy in a heartbeat.

"Julep." Miss Crosetti was standing over them. "Please get to your seat and prepare to play 'Marianne' for the challenge."

"Uh, thank you anyway, but I'm not challenging today."

"Actually, this is an all-challenge week."

"An all-what?"

"All-challenge," echoed Bernadette. "We do it once a quarter. It means everyone has to play."

At that, Julep, who was on her tippy toes, lost her balance. The weight of her steel-tipped cowboy boots sent her straight into Bernadette's music stand. It toppled and hit the stand next to it, which made that stand crash into the one next to *it,* and . . . well, six music stands and one flute section with no sense of humor later, the black metal dominoes finally stopped falling.

Wah-ahh-aaaaawk. Wah-ahh. Ahhhhhk.

"Julep!"

Wahhhhhh. Wa-wa-wahhh.

"Julep!"

Wak.

"Thank you," said Miss Crosetti, clawing at her conductor's stand. Her perky young face was all squished up like she'd guzzled a mouthful of rotten milk and was too polite to spit it out. "Ease up on your embouchure a bit, Julep. I see you're having a little trouble hitting that F."

"A little?" Eddie coughed under his breath, emptying his spit valve on her cowboy boot.

"Yuck-o." Julep wiped the side of her boot on his trumpet case. "Stop it."

"Man, Julep, your elephant didn't fart today," hooted Eddie. "It up and died."

The brass section and most of the woodwinds roared. Had she really sounded that awful?

She'd had little choice in the matter. It was either play "Marianne" and sound awful or don't play "Marianne" and get a note from Miss Crosetti to take to her parents. According to Hannah Mercks, who sat beside Julep in the trombone section, those who went home with a note never came back. Playing when you hadn't practiced in three weeks was painful. But getting kicked out of band would be far more devastating. Julep searched the sea of heads in front of her until her eyes locked onto Bernadette's. Her co-best friend gave her a thumbs-up and mouthed "good job."

Crêpe suzettes! She had been that bad. Julep wanted to melt right into the saliva-soaked green carpeting.

By the way, thank you, Bernadette, for forgetting to enlighten me about all-challenge week.

Julep kicked the base of her music stand, but she knew it wasn't Bernadette's fault. She should have practiced. She should have been ready. She tried to cheer herself up with the thought that other people in her section had struggled, too. Maybe her elephant hadn't died, after all. Maybe it was only in a coma, you know, still on life support.

"First chair, Charlie. Second chair, Julia . . ." Miss Crosetti was announcing the new order for the trumpet section.

There is no way you're going to be in the first three chairs, so don't even go there.

However, she might have a shot at fourth chair. Samantha Squires had completely butchered the melody.

Like you didn't?

She pretended she hadn't thought that.

"Third chair, Antonio."

Julep set her trumpet in the black velvet-lined case in preparation to move up two full chairs and, more importantly, eons away from Eddie Levitt's nasty tongue, body odor, and spit valve. *Fourth chair is yours.*

"Fourth chair, Samantha."

Julep's shoulders drooped.

Hang in there. You're going to get fifth chair for sure. Danny didn't make it through the whole song either. Fifth chair is SO yours.

Uh-huh. Right.

"Fifth chair, Danny."

Julep slid down until she could barely see over her music stand.

Oh, God, let me be next. Please give me sixth chair and I'll practice two hours every day for the rest of my life.

Eddie knew only two notes, neither of which was in "Marianne." It only made sense that Julep should be next in line.

"Sixth chair, Eddie."

Julep shielded her eyes with a hand.

Don't say it, Miss Crosetti. Please, don't say it. We all know who is the only miserable human being left in the trumpet section. You don't have to—

"Seventh chair, Julep."

Julep cringed, hating what was becoming a permanent attachment to her name. If she didn't do something, she was going to be known as Seventh Chair Julep for the rest of her life. Stroking the plush fabric of Harmony's skirt, she fought the overwhelming urge to run from the room. Miss Crosetti moved on to the French horns. But for Julep, the pain that went with getting stuck in last chair wrapped itself around her. As the period wore on, it tightened its hold, threatening to suffocate her. One day, she feared, it probably would.

17 DEATH BY DRAMA CLUB

After school, Julep had barely set both cowboy boots inside the cafeteria when cast and crew members bombarded her.

"The bed frame is here," said Tessa. "My dad's bringing the truck around to the back door and we're going to set everything up onstage, okay?"

"Now? I thought you were going to do that this morning before school."

"My dad couldn't do it then. He can now."

What could Julep say? She gave Tessa the go-ahead, though all that hammering was certainly going to put a crimp in their run-through.

Kathleen was next. "I've got all the mattress covers ready. What should I do with them?"

"Uh, well . . . do you have them on the mattresses?"

"No."

"It wouldn't hurt."

She wrinkled her forehead. ""Why would it hurt? They're just covers."

"Just talking to her hurts." Bernadette giggled into her ear while they watched Kathleen trot away.

Julep crossed one amber eye and then, just as quickly, uncrossed it. "Bernadette, I'm sorry about what I said at lunch. I didn't mean—"

"Me, too. I'll try not to, you know, soak everybody, in the future."

Julep laughed. "I never said you soaked everybody. Not even close. It was a dumb thing to say anyway. Can we erase it?"

Bernadette slid a hand across her forehead to signal she was wiping Julep's words from her memory. Her gesture meant that Julep's comment was not only forgiven, but forgotten. "So what do you think?" Bernadette twirled in her costume, a long plum-colored satin gown with flowing sleeves. "My grandma made it. She's going to make my crown, too, out of purple carnations and baby's breath on Saturday afternoon so it'll be fresh for the performance."

"Sounds perfect."

"Perfect enough for . . ." She bent toward Julep. ". . . a princess?"

Middle-school gossip traveled faster than a moon rocket. "You know about Danica?"

"Everybody knows. What are you going to do?"

Julep bit her lower lip. "Nothing yet. I'd like to see if I can straighten things out with her first before I give her part to someone else."

Bernadette said that sounded fair. "Would it be all right if I filled in for Danica during the dress rehearsal? I know all her lines, and that way you can see how I would do as the princess. I don't mean to pressure you or anything."

"Okay. Just for today, though—"

"Julep!" Jillian skidded to a halt. "I forgot my hat."

"Don't worry about it."

"I can't act without my hat."

"Trust me, you can't act *with* one," cracked Betsy, flinging an arm around Julep's neck and steering her toward a corner. "Danica's not coming back."

"How do you know?"

"I'm her best friend." There was that slimy snake of a grin again. "I know."

Julep wriggled out of her grasp. "We'll see."

Betsy's jaw tightened, but her tone remained sugary. "So until you *see*, what are you going to do? You can't have a dress rehearsal without a princess. It makes sense that I should be the one to take over the lead."

Behind them, Bernadette cleared her throat. "Julep already said *I* could read the part of the princess today."

"You?" The sweetness in Betsy's voice dissolved. "Julep, have you totally blown a brain fuse? I know you're friends, but you can't let Spit Chick be the princess. It's not right."

"What did you say?" Bernadette's lips had disappeared into her mouth. Her nostrils were quivering. The tiny vein in the middle of her forehead was bulging.

Uh-oh.

Julep took a full step back.

"Spit Chick? *Spit Chick?*" Bernadette curled her hands in.

"Spitting is not always something a person can help, unlike being a vicious, two-faced, backstabbing jerk-and-a-half, which is completely optional."

Betsy rolled her neck around. It was one of her idiotic relaxation exercises that she'd picked up from a library book on acting. "What's your problem?"

"You. My problem is you, Betsy," said Bernadette, a torpedo of saliva shooting out her front teeth on the second syllable of the gosling's name. It fell short of its target's chest by less than a foot. Darn!

Bernadette, however, wasn't remotely close to being finished. "Julep was there when you trashed Danica in the girls' bathroom. She heard you say how the way Danica drools over Ethan makes you sick and how Danica overacts and how the only reason she got the part was because of her long hair . . ."

A certain photographic memory had struck again.

Julep was feeling a bit light-headed, probably because it had been more than three hours since lunch, and even then, she'd only had a few bites of her mom's poisonous pita pocket.

"She heard you say how if your hair had been past your shoulders that part would have been yours. So you'd better watch your step, because Julep could go to Danica anytime and tell her the truth about you."

Betsy turned on Julep, her eyes ablaze. "What? Did you really hide out in the bathroom to listen in on us?"

"Not on purpose. I was sort of . . . there when you were there." The left side of her face and eight out of ten fingers were tingling. She was also having trouble breathing. "I . . . I . . . I . . ."

Suddenly the cafeteria floor was rolling beneath her cowboy boots. Everyone around her was swimming in a checkerboard ocean. Julep felt seasick. In the distance, the Lunch Monster was navigating her cranberry-sofa pirate ship through choppy black-and-white waters.

Somehow, she didn't know how, Julep kept her head above the stormy sea. She tripped up the stage steps and across the hardwood floor. Tearing a path through the red velvet curtain, Julep raced down the backstage hallway. She latched onto the first doorknob she came to and, sliding on the soles of her boots, flung herself through the door. Julep slammed the door. She blocked it with her body. Huffing, she let her head fall back. She was in the prop room, where all of the set pieces, furniture, and decorations were stored. It was a quiet place, a good place to rest. Julep shut her eyes. She took several deep breaths. When, at last, she felt the blood began to circulate normally through her limbs, her eyelids fluttered open.

"Ah!" She inhaled the word, startled to see Millie and Trig gawking at her.

The overhead light was off. The room was lit only by a square of sunlight shining down through the ceiling skylight.

"Sorry," said Julep, peering into the shadows. "I didn't know anyone was—what is that?" She tried, but couldn't recall any scenes that required a pale pink papier-mâché ball like the one Millie was holding. Beside her, Trig was poised over the ball with a carving knife.

"What *is* that?" Julep asked again.

Neither of them answered. Neither moved.

Squinting, Julep could see the top of the ball was covered in wavy orange squiggles. On the side facing her, someone had painted two golden eyeballs and tapped dozens of tiny brown dots over pink cheeks and a pug nose with a dent at the end—

Ohmygosh! It's me!

A violent shudder tore through her head (the real one, not the fake one). Julep let out a whimper as it occurred to her that what she had stumbled into was far worse than what she had just escaped. It was obvious what was going on here. Trig and Millie were practicing to—

Kill me! They're going to kill me.

Was she that bad of a director?

Inching backward, Julep felt something pointy dig into her spine. She cried out, her fingers fumbling for the door. Trig's arm was still in the air, his hand tightly gripping the knife, when he swung to face her. Suddenly a beam of sunlight shot through the skylight. The silver blade reflected it directly into Julep's eyes. She was blinded!

In flashes of black and gold, Julep saw Trig coming toward her. Behind her, she wildly lashed out her arm, searching for the doorknob. Where *was* the door?

"Trig," she croaked, trying to blink away the starburst. "What are you doing?"

Trig's eyes were hidden by the brim of his baseball cap. She could not see him. She could not reach him. This was how it was going to end. She was going to die in the Heatherwood prop room in her frilly red shirt, cowboy boots, and her sister's suede skirt.

Oh, no! Harmony is going to kill me if I get blood on this skirt.

Miraculously, Julep's fingers closed around the brass doorknob. She yanked it, and bolted down the narrow hallway as fast her boots could carry her.

"Julep? You in here?" It was Trig!

Cowering in stall six, Julep let out a silent scream. Didn't he know boys weren't allowed in the girls' bathroom, especially to chop them into itty-bitty pieces?

Don't move. Don't breathe. Don't even think.

"She's not here," said another voice.

"Bernadette!" shrieked Julep. "Call the police. Call nine-one-one. Trig's trying to kill me."

"Told you," said Trig.

"Julep," said Bernadette sternly. "Come out here."

She's in on the plot, too. Betsy has nothing on these two. Talk about backstabbing friends!

Her knees weak, Julep crept back until she felt the cold porcelain against her palms. Taking cover, she hunched down next to the toilet. She plucked the spare roll of tissue paper off the shelf behind her, ready to chuck it at her *former* co-best friends if necessary. She wished she had a more deadly weapon than T.P., but beggars couldn't be choosers. "Why couldn't you stay at your table and sleep?" Julep yelled. "At least I knew where you were and what you were doing then: nothing!"

Trig moaned. "If you'd let me—"

"Go away. I'll scream."

"Julep, wait—"

"Yeeeeeeee-aaaaahhhhhhhh!"

When Julep's screech had finished ricocheting off the walls, she heard Bernadette say softly to Trig, "Maybe you'd better go."

"Yeah. Guess so. So this is what it's like in here. Huh. You always wonder. It's a lot nicer than the guys' room. Smells better. Your sink isn't broken either—"

"Trig?"

"Right. Tell her the murderer will call her tonight, okay?"

"I think she heard."

Eee-yoh. The door closed. The girls were alone.

Kneeling down next to the toilet, Julep had a clear line of sight underneath the blue stall door. Soon, Bernadette's purple-and-white tennis shoes appeared. Julep watched them kick at the hem of the plum satin gown as they paced back and forth. Clutching her roll of toilet paper, Julep knew she would only have one shot at beaning Bernadette if her former friend succeeded in getting past her last line of defense: the sticky door. Julep decided to aim for her glasses. It was her only chance.

"Julep, I want you to listen carefully." Bernadette was calm. Too calm. Horror-movie calm. "Trig is not trying to kill you."

"You weren't there," shouted Julep. "I saw it . . . big papier-mâché head of me . . . huge knife . . . Trig was about to stab the head. He was practicing for the real thing, Bernadette—me!"

"Okay, okay. Take it easy. What you saw *was* a papier-mâché copy of your head, and yes, Trig was about to slice into you, I mean it—"

"I knew it!"

"But see, the head was for you."

Julep frowned. What the heck did that mean?

"Millie made it," Bernadette continued. "Trig was cutting an opening in the top for her so she could fill it with Reese's Pieces. *Reese's Pieces.* Get it?"

It was Julep's favorite candy. So what?

"We were going to give it to you onstage after the performance. It was supposed to be a surprise thank-you gift for saving the play and being our director." Bernadette sighed, digging her toe into the floor. "Some surprise."

Was it true? Or was this merely a trick to get her to come out of the stall? Julep supposed it was *possible* she could have misunderstood the scene in the prop room. Now that she thought about, Trig didn't seem much like a crazed murderer a few moments ago.

"Julep?"

Silence.

"You believe me, don't you?"

Unfortunately, she did. Julep had not only ruined the play, but now she had blown her surprise gift as well. The adrenaline rush draining from her, she released her ammunition. It bounced once then rolled under the partition into stall number five.

Bernadette's hair hit the floor. She was trying to peek under the door. "Are you okay?"

"Yeah."

"Is there anything I can—?"

"No. Yes." She sank down. "Go away so I can drown in my embarrassment."

"Julep, it's not that bad."

"Please, Bernadette." Julep rested her weary head against the blue wall. She wasn't in the mood for her regular dose of sympathy from the More Girl. "Leave me alone?"

Julep watched her friend's tennis shoes circle clockwise, then turn and do another full circle counterclockwise. When they began to slowly walk in a straight line, a tear rolled down a freckled cheek. She didn't want Bernadette to go. Not really.

Eee-yoh.

Julep sprang to her feet. "Berna—"

Woooooosh! Julep stretched for the door and felt a sharp tug on her waist. She swung her head around. The seat was up. The evil red eye was blinking. The smart toilet had a firm grip on the back of her skirt. There was no escape. The whirlwind of water was pulling her in!

18 One Little Word

Nooooooooo!" screamed Julep, fighting against the powerful force of the flush. She clung to the only thing she could: the round plastic four-roll toilet-paper dispenser mounted on the sidewall. She heard the sounds, the horrible sounds, of plastic snapping, fabric ripping, and boots skidding. Julep knew she couldn't hold on very long. The suction was too strong. When her fingers finally gave out, she was swept off her feet and dragged backward. She was going in! Julep bumped her elbow, a knee, and her right hip before landing hard, her backside in the toilet.

Splash!

Blub. Blub. Gurgle.

Blub.

In less than fifteen seconds, the violent hurricane was over. Water was flowing over the top of the seat. Squeezing the outside of the bowl with her wet forearms, Julep managed to hoist herself up onto the edge. "Stupid smart toilet," she hissed at the red eye. It was no longer blinking, its steady beam mocking her. Julep's hip was sore, her elbow was growing a bump, and more parts than she wanted to admit were soaked in toilet water (yuck-o!). But otherwise she was okay. Julep tried to stand up, but was yanked back into the white porcelain bowl of death.

Rats!

The skirt was wedged in the drain. Julep reached behind her, gathered a handful of suede, and gently tugged. It didn't budge. She pulled a bit harder. Same result. The skirt was lodged in the throat of the smart toilet—tightly, cruelly, and permanently lodged. She couldn't put the seat down because her skirt was in the way, so Julep carefully balanced herself on the outside edge of the bowl. After she had caught her breath, she dared to glance back. The soft, parchment fabric was now stiff and wet and heavy. And ruined. Harmony was going to freak out when she saw this. *If* she ever saw it. What a nightmare! Julep looked around. What in the world was she supposed to do now?

Bam. Bam. Bam.

Someone was at her stall door!

"Uh, yes?" she said lightly, smoothing down her wizzle hair and casually tapping her cowboy boots against the tile floor. "I'm a little busy in here."

"Is there a problem?" It was the Lunch Monster! "I heard noises."

Julep licked her lips. "I'll be out in a minute."

"Are you sure there's nothing wrong?"

"Um . . . yeah . . ." She crossed her legs. "Everything's, uh, fine."

Are you serious? You're stuck in a middle-school toilet. It doesn't get any more un-fine that this.

The thing of it was it was just *so* hard to say.

So don't. Sit here clogging the smart toilet for the rest of your life. Pretend you've got all the answers when all you've really got is Jiffy Pop hair, soggy undies, and a bruised rear end. Some big-time director you are.

The Lunch Monster was almost to the door when she heard it. It was barely a word—more like a whimper, really.

"Help?"

A pair of size-ten orthopedic shoes stopped. An aqua dress with approximately 26,425 bunnies swung to a standstill. And Mrs. Flaskin, who never smiled, finally did.

6:19 p.m.   Mood: Amazed

Dear Amelia:

W.A.A.D! I don't know where to begin! Here are the highlights:

Worst moment: When the stupid smart toilet at school tried to
                 eat me! I was wearing Harmony's suede skirt.
                 After some heavy-duty plunging, Mr. Havlett
                 fished out the skirt. It's definitely toast. Water
                 and suede do not mix. Harmony isn't talking to
                 me. I told her I had only promised not to get
                 anything ON the skirt. I'd never said anything
                 about getting it jammed IN anything. P.L.E.,
                 huh? I tried to explain it was an accident.
                 Harmony yelled, "You're the accident!" and
                 slammed her bedroom door in my face.

Best moment: Mrs. Flaskin to the rescue! You should have
               seen her crash through the sticky stall door to
               save me.

Worst outfit: A tie between my ladybug underwear with my
               cowboy boots, which I was wearing when I had to
               unzip the skirt and leave it behind in the toilet,
               and Mrs. Flaskin's HUMONGOUS cardigan sweater,
               which she let me wrap around myself once I got
               out of the skirt.

Best outfit: Bernadette's jeans. Fooled you! You thought I
                    was going to say Harmony's skirt. After the
                    T.S.I. Bernadette let me borrow her jeans to
                    wear for the rest of the day (she wore her
                    costume home). The jeans were a little too big in
                    the waist and a little too long, but I didn't care.
                    I loved wearing them because they were
                    Bernadette's. What can I say? She is still my
                    diamond.

Biggest Surprise: Mrs. Flaskin told me (as I was putting on her
                    sweater) I was doing a good job as director! I
                    told her I was having a little trouble controlling
                    everyone. She said she knew. She said she
                    would be happy to help me. It was a huge relief!
                    Mrs. Flaskin isn't so scary once you figure out
                    which eye to look at. The right one. I think.

Gotta scoot. I have one more thing to do tonight. Wish me
patience. Wish me success. Wish me a calm tummy.

                        C.Y.L.,
                        Julep

        P.S. The rumor about Mrs. Flaskin having no
        teeth isn't true. She's got them all right.

Julep's Decoder Page
TOP SECRET STUFF!

W.A.A.D.: What an Amazing Day

P.L.E.: Pretty Lame Excuse

T.S.I.: Toilet Sucking Incident

PROTECTED BY 24-HOUR STATE-OF-THE-ART SECURITY CAMERAS (AND BAXTER III, MY GOLDFISH)

19 A Director, At Last

Hello?"

"Danica? Hi, it's Julep. O'Toole. Hi."

Danica didn't respond. But she didn't hang up either.

"I'm . . . um . . . calling about the play. About you quitting, I mean."

"What about it?"

"I was wondering why you quit."

"You know why."

"I don't, Danica. Really I don't."

"I have nothing to say." Her voice broke, which meant she had plenty to say.

"If something happened that you want to tell me about—"

"No."

"No something didn't happen or no you don't want to talk about it?"

Danica didn't answer. But she sniffled. Twice. Was she crying?

Julep pressed on. "If I said something to hurt your feelings—"

"You mean, besides telling people I have dyslexia? Besides telling people I am such a ditz you are going to have to make big cue cards for the play because I'm too stupid to memorize my lines? Is that what you mean?"

Julep was astonished. She could barely gasp, "I never said that!"

"Yeah. Right."

Julep knew what dyslexia was. It meant a person had difficulty writing and/or reading. Julep's cousin Kiki had it. To Kiki's brain, some letters appeared backward or upside down. She often had a hard time telling the difference between letters that looked similar, like *d*'s and *b*'s. Based on what she saw at school, Julep would never have guessed that Danica had dyslexia, too.

"I don't get it. You always get A's on the vocab quizzes in English," said Julep.

"I do all right with spelling and writing. But I have trouble with reading—remembering what I've read and making it stay in my head. It gets worse when I'm nervous. What I don't know is how you found out about it, Julep. I've only told a few of my friends."

"That's just it. I'm telling you I *didn't* know. And even if I had, I would never have made fun of you for it." Scratching the hairline above her forehead, Julep said, "If that's the kind of person you think I am, then you don't know me very well."

The line was quiet.

That was the whole problem, wasn't it? Danica *didn't* know her. Not really.

"Let me make it very clear so in the future you won't forget," said Julep, itching her temple. Her Follicles of Fury were going full throttle. "I don't tease people, because I know how crummy it feels when somebody picks on you . . . like for your hair or your freckles. It hurts. I'm telling you I'm not . . ." She was so furious she could hardly think. "I'm not . . . not . . ."

"Betsy?"

Julep meant to say something like "I'm not the kind of girl who puts other people down to make myself feel more important." But Danica had, in one word, said it so much better.

Julep took a slow breath to calm down. "Betsy told you I said those things about you, didn't she?"

"Yeah," said Danica, her voice husky.

"I figured." You can sure learn a lot about people by hiding out in the girls' bathroom. "She's not much of a friend, if you ask me," Julep said boldly. "She wants your part in the play, you know."

"I know." Danica grunted. "Maybe she should have it. It was silly of me to think I could actually do it. When I auditioned, it seemed so cool to be onstage and have everyone watch me. Then I got the part and realized I was going to be up onstage where everyone was going to be watching me. I guess I kind of freaked."

Julep understood. Sometimes, there was nothing worse than getting everything you wanted.

"I'm really sorry, Julep. I thought I could do it."

Cradling the phone against her shoulder, Julep got up off her bed. "What if we could prompt you during the play without anyone noticing? Would you come back?"

"That's a big if."

"But if I found a way, would you come back?"

"No big cue cards, right?"

"No," vowed Julep.

"I don't know. I've already missed dress rehearsal."

"We postponed it until Friday." Julep didn't say why.

"You did?" There was a tinge of hope in her voice. It rapidly faded. "What if I take one look at the audience and my dyslexic brain twits out? What if I mess up in front of everyone?"

"What if you do? Even when you flub all your lines, Danica, you're still a million times better than everybody else. You know why?"

"Why?"

"Because you have emo-o-o-o-tion."

Danica laughed, but Julep was serious. How could she make the Head Goose understand that they didn't need her to be perfect, they just needed *her*?

"We can find a way to make it work. I know we can," said Julep. "Danica, please don't let your head talk your heart out of it." She crossed her fingers and toes, and placed one ankle over the other—the rarely used and reserved for desperate causes only quintuple cross! Danica had to come back to the play. She just had to.

A charm bracelet jangled. "You sure don't give up easily, do you?"

Julep had done it! Danica was back in the play. Julep twirled around and around and around on her apricot carpet. Not to make life a blur. To celebrate it.

When Julep trotted downstairs, Harmony and Kyle were hunched over the kitchen table doing homework. Julep said hi.

Kyle said hi back. Harmony didn't look up. She was still not speaking to Julep. This shutout, Julep knew, could last a long while. When it came to the silent treatment, nobody had more stamina than Harmony. Julep opened the refrigerator door.

Harmony turned to her boyfriend. "Tell my sister that we're not supposed to touch the key lime pie. That's for Mom's dessert night at the museum tomorrow."

Kyle raised one eyebrow. "But she's . . . you want me to—"

"Tell her, please."

He sighed. "Julep, you're not supposed to eat any of the—"

"I heard," Julep shot. "You can tell *my* sister that I already knew that."

Kyle had caught on. He went back to his book.

"Well?" Harmony was glaring at Kyle, tapping her pencil against the edge of the table.

"You heard what Julep said," he said firmly, but not meanly. "And don't put me in the middle of whatever this is."

Julep pulled her head out of the fridge. Were her ears malfunctioning? Had Kyle Patterson just stood his ground with the beautiful, popular, and enchanting Harmony O'Toole? Her sister, who was used to getting her way, must be in shock right now. Julep reached for an apple and caught the look on her sister's face. Yep. Harmony was fruiting out all right.

Cooper marched into the kitchen, dragging his stuffed bunny, Fred. "Trig's here."

"It's done!" Trig appeared, holding a square blue Tupperware container.

"What's done?" asked Kyle.

"His new concoction," explained Julep. "Trig's a chef."

Harmony flipped her hair back. "That's debatable."

Trig popped off the lid. "Who wants to be the first to try one?"

Harmony, Julep, and Kyle pointed to the kid hugging a one-eyed, hairless bunny.

"Cool!" Cooper stuck a grimy hand into the plastic box and scooped out a golf-ball-size blob rolled in what looked like crushed graham crackers. Or cereal. Or some kind of nuts.

Julep did a double take. Peanuts? She flung her apple on the counter. Lunging for her brother, Julep knocked the cluster out of his hand a split second before he bit into it. It fell on the floor and broke apart.

"What did you do that for, Jules?"

She pointed at the pieces. "You're allergic to peanuts."

"Those aren't peanuts," said Trig, frowning at the mess. "They're cornflakes."

"Oh," said Julep sheepishly. "Then they're okay."

"Maybe you'd better tell us what's in it," said Harmony. "To be safe."

"It's everything you'd eat for breakfast all rolled into one. There's yogurt, eggs, orange juice, toast and butter, sausage, and cornflakes." Trig beamed. "I call them Maxwell's Mighty Mouthfuls."

Cooper looked to Julep for approval. As far as she could tell, there was nothing there that would cause an extreme food reaction or set off an asthma attack. The toast could be a small issue. Cooper had trouble digesting wheat products, which was more of a sensitivity thing than an actual allergy. Even so, Julep didn't see where a bite or two of Trig's concoction would hurt. She gave him the go-ahead.

Cooper reached in for another lopsided ball. They watched him take a bite. After a few chews, he made a face. Not a good face. Fred hit the floor. Cooper raced for the bathroom.

"Pass," said Harmony, when Trig offered her the Tupperware container.

"In a minute," said Julep. She was taking her time ripping off paper towels to clean up the floor.

Kyle, however, couldn't resist Trig's one-of-a-kind recipe. Bravely, he plucked out one of the largest clusters then surprised them all by popping the whole thing in his mouth! Julep gasped. Harmony shrieked. Cooper, who had come back in the kitchen in time to witness it, smacked the side of his head.

Cheeks bulging, Kyle bit down. Almost instantly, tears sprang to his eyes. He started to chew slowly. Then a little faster. And faster still. From the neck up, he began to turn red, and not a fever-flush shade of red either, but a bluish-purplish-maroon color. Yet Kyle didn't run to the bathroom. He kept right on chewing and tearing up and reddening. Would he ever swallow? Could he swallow?

At last, there rose a noise from the depths of his throat. "Plath."

"He's trying to say something," cried Harmony.

"I think he's going to hurl!" yelled Cooper.

"Plath-noba-fee."

Trig wrinkled his brow. "Was that *thee*? Or *fee*?"

"We don't understand you," Harmony patted Kyle's back. "Do you need something?"

"Probably a drink," guessed Julep, scurrying for the refrigerator. Harmony grabbed a glass out of the cupboard and slid it down the counter. Julep poured the milk. Like an Olympic relay runner grabbing the baton, Kyle swiped the glass from Julep's hand. Throwing his head back, he chugged the whole thing in four gulps and five seconds flat. Reeling, Kyle held on to the counter and tried to catch his breath. It took a few minutes for his face to find its way back from octopus red to a fleshy pink.

"So?" Trig stuck his thumbs in his belt loops. "What did you think?"

Four sets of eyes stared at Trig in bewilderment, then swung to hear Kyle's review.

With a nod to Julep, Kyle said, in a raspy voice, "Plan Number Three."

They put it to a vote. It was four to one—Maxwell's Mighty Mouthfuls had to drown. And they had to drown now.

From her spot atop the big granite rock overlooking the pond, Julep placed her left hand on her heart. "We salute you, O—Trig, what's in it again?"

"Yogurt, eggs, orange juice, toast and butter, sausage, and cornflakes," came the sullen reply from behind her. Trig had refused to participate in the execution of his beloved recipe.

Julep munched her bottom lip. The list sounded oddly familiar.

With Cooper on the shore to her left and Harmony and Kyle

on her right, Julep started again. "We salute you, O yogurt, eggs, orange juice, toast and butter, sausage, and cornflakes, for giving your life for Trig's horrible concoction." Julep could not shake the feeling that she *had* come across these items somewhere before. But where?

"Now what?" Harmony hissed to Kyle during the moment of silence.

"We throw it in on Julep's command. Aim for the middle."

"Ready?" Julep shouted.

Harmony glanced at the cluster in her hand. "You know, in theory, it wasn't a bad idea putting yogurt, eggs, butter, toast, and—"

"Aim!" yelled Julep.

They cocked their arms. Trig clamped his eyes shut.

As she opened her mouth to signal them to send their clusters skyward, it finally dawned on Julep where she'd seen those ingredients. The Internet. Yes! That was it. Trig's concoction might not be edible, but that didn't mean it wasn't valuable.

"Halt!" shouted Julep.

Four heads swiveled her way. Trig opened one eye. Was it true? Had his recipe received an official pardon?

"You're supposed to say 'fire,'" said Harmony.

"Yeah, Jules, what's the deal?" said Cooper, cycling his arms to keep from falling into the pond.

Julep scampered down from her perch. "Everybody, give me your food," she commanded, holding out the front of her sweatshirt to make a big basket. "Come on, dump your Mighty Mouthfuls in here."

"You're not going to eat them, are you?" asked Kyle, tossing his chunk in.

"Nope. I've got bigger plans."

Trig liked the sound of that. "Bigger plans?"

"Like what?" asked Cooper, handing over his cluster.

"Freckles."

"Huh?" The three boys were lost.

Harmony, however, was not confused at all. "Oh, no," she moaned. "Not again."

20   Life Off-Script

Julep ran her hand along the inseam of the red velvet curtain. The stage was dark. Yet she could easily make out the shapes of papier-mâché daffodils, bushes, and trees lining the pathway to the castle door. For the castle walls, the stage crew had nailed together several large boards, painting them to resemble distressed gray brick. Inside the castle, the giant four-poster bed was piled high with mattresses and feather beds in every imaginable pattern, shape, and color—bumblebee stripes, jewel-toned plaids, neon geometrics, leopard prints. Even better, when Danica climbed up the five-foot ladder to the top of the heap, it would look to the audience as if she were stretching out on top of all of that bedding. In truth, her weight would be supported by a sturdy platform hidden between the mattresses that Tessa's dad had devised and built.

"Does everything look okay?" Tessa had joined Julep in the wings.

"It looks great," Julep whispered, grinning. "I can't believe we finished in time."

"I couldn't have done it without everybody pitching in to work overtime, especially Trig."

"Trig?"

Tessa bobbed her head. "He was here until nine last night, then came back this morning and worked all day."

"Trig Maxwell?" Julep had to confirm it.

"Looks like our bear came out of hibernation in the nick of time."

"I'll say."

Tessa parted the velvet curtain. "Wow! It's really filling up out there. I'd better go set up some extra chairs."

Julep looked out, too. Suddenly the two tacos she'd had for dinner began doing the tango in her stomach. An endless thread of parents, grandparents, teachers, and kids was filing into the cafeteria. People were talking, milling about, and fanning themselves with the programs. Glancing at the folded paper in her hand, Julep still found it hard to believe that it was her sister who had come to her rescue.

"Get off the computer." Harmony had stood over her last night. "Your time is up."

"You're talking to me now?"

"Only in emergencies. Now get off. I have to e-mail Marielle."

"I'm almost done. One more minute."

Harmony tapped her watch. "No more minutes."

Julep clicked her mouse, sending her work to their printer. Harmony picked up the page that slid out of the machine. "This is the program for the play? This is what you're handing out to everyone?"

"Yes."

"Noooooo."

"Yeeeeees."

Harmony pointed to the ballerina on the page. "It's all wrong, Julep. This is for a dance recital."

Julep lifted a sore shoulder. "It's all I could find."

"The font is too wide."

"It looks all right to me—"

"All the names are crooked on the inside. You didn't tab, did you?"

"Tab?"

"Get up." Harmony rolled her silver-blue eyes. "I'll do it."

In twenty minutes, Harmony had found a color illustration of a castle with a drawbridge. She placed it on the front of the program. Above it, in an Old English font style, she typed *The Princess and The Pea, a Production of Heatherwood Middle School.* A few clicks later, she had fixed Julep's crooked columns so all the names of the cast and crew appeared in neat, straight rows. Harmony's finger hit the print button as their mother came into the family room and asked if Julep was ready to go to the copy store to print the play programs.

"We're almost done," said Julep, watching the whirring printer spew out the new and improved program.

"It's nice to see the two of you have made up," said their mom, going into the hall to get her purse.

"Officially, I'm still not talking to you," corrected Harmony. "Just so you know, I'm going to be mad for the rest of this week."

"Okay."

"And maybe next week, too."

"Okay."

"I probably won't come to your play."

That one had stung.

"Five minutes, everybody." Millie's voice echoed down the backstage hallway. "Five minutes."

The tacos in Julep's stomach picked up their feet or beans or whatever.

"Feel my hands." Danica grabbed Julep's fingers. "They're frozen solid."

Julep rubbed Danica's hands to warm them. "Remember, if you forget a line—"

"Jingle my charm bracelet once and Bernadette will whisper it to me." She held up her arm. "My bracelet—!"

"Is on your other wrist," said Julep, turning Danica's palm over for her.

Danica probed Julep's eyes. "I hope Bernadette doesn't—"

"She won't." Julep had never been more sure of anything in her life.

The Head Goose did her bobblehead impression again.

Julep released her hands. "Good luck, Danica."

"No!" cried Cherry Anne, coming between them. "You never say good luck to an actor. It's bad luck."

"It is?"

"What do you say?"

"Break a leg."

"That seems kind of mean," said Julep.

Cherry Anne gave her a glare.

"Okay. Break a leg, Danica."

"Thanks. I think."

Julep saw Bernadette hurrying down the narrow backstage hall toward her. She was wearing her plum satin gown with a pair of white ballet slippers. Bernadette's mom had braided the sides of her daughter's hair, then wrapped the braids around her head and pinned them up in back. A crown of lavender carnations and baby's breath rested on the braids. Her cheeks flushed, Bernadette looked anxious and happy. And beautiful.

Bernadette lifted her chin. "Is it too much?"

"Is what too much?"

"Shoot, you can't even see it? I put a whole bunch of silver glitter lotion on my face. I wanted to really sparkle tonight."

Julep grinned and told her the truth. "You do."

"Two minutes!" Millie was calling. "Places, everybody."

"Stick by her," Julep said to Bernadette.

Her friend wriggled her nose to slide her glasses up. "I'm glue."

Peeking through the curtain, Julep's eyes bounced from head to head until, at last, she spotted the twisty top of her mother's reddish-brown bun. Her family was sitting about halfway back near the windows. She wouldn't have seen Cooper at all but for the wispy cowlick on top of his head standing straight up. Aunt Ivy sat beside Cooper. Next to Aunt Ivy was—could it be? Julep squinted to be sure, that the sun-streaked head belonged to her sister. It did! Harmony had come, after all. Julep couldn't tell for sure, but it looked like her sister was holding a bunch of yellow roses. Julep smiled. Something told her the flowers were for her. Kyle was seated next to her sister.

It was already after seven and people were still coming in. At the back of the auditorium, Mrs. Flaskin was helping Tessa set up more chairs.

"Let's wait a couple more minutes so everyone can get seated," Julep instructed Robbie, who was manning the curtain and lights. He nodded.

Julep crumpled her program. This was it!

Soon, Heatherwood Middle School's production of *The Princess and the Pea* would get under way. The second it began, Julep's job as director would end. Anything could happen. A certain lopsided papier-mâché tree might tip over in the middle of Act II the way it had done during dress rehearsal. Calvin could make good on his threat to wear a Santa hat and humongous red boxer shorts (where was he anyway?). Onstage, with everyone watching, Danica might finally find someone to trust, maybe even herself. Anything could happen.

It was scary, the not knowing. Yet it was kind of exciting, too.

"Dim the lights," Julep whispered to Robbie.

The cafeteria went dark. The backstage lights went off, too, but for a single lightbulb next to Robbie. As Julep's eyes adjusted, she saw the silhouettes of Bernadette, Danica, Ethan, Cherry Anne, and the rest of the cast. They stood still and silent in the shadows, waiting for their cue. The audience grew quiet. A hand on her thumping heart, Julep took a ragged breath. There was only one thing left for the director to say. And so Julep said it.

"Curtain up."